JUNGLE

On the

Presented to

Alex

June 2013

[signature] RECTOR

The Lord bless you and keep you.
Numbers 6:24

②

JUNGLE DOCTOR
On the Hop

Paul White

CF4•K

10 9 8 7 6 5 4 3

Jungle Doctor on the Hop ISBN 978-1-84550-297-3
© Copyright 1988 Paul White
First published 1957, reprinted 1963, 1966
Paperback edition 1972, revised edition 1988.

Published in 2007 and reprinted in 2008 and 2010
by Christian Focus Publications, Geanies House, Fearn, Tain,
Ross-shire, IV20 1TW, Scotland, U.K.
Fact files: © Copyright Christian Focus Publications
Paul White Productions,
4/1-5 Busaco Road, Marsfield, NSW 2122, Australia

Cover design: Daniel van Straaten
Cover illustration: Craig Howarth
Interior illustrations: Graham Wade
Printed and bound by Norhaven A/S, Denmark

Since the Jungle Doctor books were first published there have been a number of Jungle Doctors working in Mvumi Hospital, Tanzania, East Africa - some Australian, some British, a West Indian and a number of East African Jungle Doctors to name but a few.

African words are used throughout the book, but explained at least once within the text. A glossary of the more important words is included at the front of the book along with a key character index.

CONTENTS

Fact File: Paul White

Born in 1910 in Bowral, New South Wales, Australia, Paul had Africa in his blood for as long as he could remember. His father captured his imagination with stories of his experiences in the Boer War which left an indelible impression. His father died of meningitis in army camp in 1915, and he was left an only child without his father at five years of age. He inherited his father's storytelling gift along with a mischievous sense of humour.

He committed his life to Christ as a sixteen-year-old school-boy and studied medicine as the next step towards missionary work in Africa. Paul and his wife, Mary, left Sydney, with their small son, David, for Tanganyika in 1938. He always thought of this as his life's work but Mary's severe illness forced their early return to Sydney in 1941. Their daughter, Rosemary, was born while they were overseas.

Within weeks of landing in Sydney, Paul was invited to begin a weekly radio broadcast which spread throughout Australia as the Jungle Doctor Broadcasts - the last of these was aired in 1985. The weekly scripts for these programmes became the raw material for the Jungle Doctor hospital stories - a series of twenty books.

Paul always said he preferred life to be a 'mixed grill' and so it was: writing, working as a Rheumatologist, public speaking, involvement with many Christian organisations, adapting the fable stories into multiple forms (comic books, audio cassettes, filmstrips), radio and television, and sharing his love of birds with others by producing bird song cassettes - and much more...

The books in part or whole have been translated into 109 languages.

Paul saw that although his plan to work in Africa for life was turned on its head, in God's better planning he was able to reach more people by coming home than by staying. It was a great joy to meet people over the years who told him they were on their way overseas to work in mission because of the books.

Paul's wife, Mary, died after a long illness in 1970. He married Ruth and they had the joy of working together on many new projects. He died in 1992 but the stories and fables continue to attract an enthusiastic readership of all ages.

Fact file: Tanzania

The Jungle Doctor books are based on Paul White's missionary experiences in Tanzania. Today many countries in Africa have gained their independence. This has resulted in a series of name changes. Tanganyika is one such country that has now changed its name to Tanzania.

The name Tanganyika is no longer used formally for the territory. Instead the name Tanganyika is used almost exclusively to mean the lake.

During World War I, what was then Tanganyika came under British military rule. On December 9, 1961 it became independent. In 1964, it joined with the islands of Zanzibar to form the United Republic of Tanganyika and Zanzibar, changed later in the year to the United Republic of Tanzania.

It is not only its name that has changed, this area of Africa has gone through many changes since the Jungle Doctor books were first written. Africa itself has changed. Many of the same diseases raise their heads, but treatments have advanced. However new diseases come to take their place and the work goes on.

Missions throughout Africa are often now run by African Christians and not solely by foreign nationals. There are still the same problems to overcome however. The message of the gospel thankfully never changes and brings hope to those who listen and obey. *The Jungle Doctor* books are about this work to bring health and wellbeing to Africa as well as the good news of Jesus Christ and salvation.

Fact File: Plague

The plague is one of the oldest identifiable diseases known to man and is still a major problem in many countries around the world. It is still widely distributed in the tropics and subtropics and in warmer areas of temperate countries.

The three most common forms of plague are:

Bubonic - an infection of the lymph nodes.

Pneumonic - an infection of the lungs.

Septicemic - an infection of the blood.

Plague is essentially a disease that is spread by wild rodents, one rodent to another. However it is the fleas that are on these rodents that harbour the parasites that actually cause the disease. The disease is then spread to humans either by the bite of infected fleas or when handling other people who have been infected. When a plague victim with pneumonia coughs, microscopic droplets carrying the infection move through the air. Anyone who breathes in these particles can catch the disease. An epidemic may be started this way.

If the disease remains untreated deaths may reach high levels. When rapidly diagnosed and promptly treated, plague may be successfully managed with antibiotics. Modern antibiotics are effective against plague, but if an infected person is not treated promptly, the disease is likely to cause illness or death.

Fact File: Words

WORDS TO ADD EXPRESSION AND EMPHASIS:
Eheh, Heh, Hongo, Hueegh, Koh, Kumbe, Naugh, Ngheeh, Yoh.

TANZANIAN LANGUAGES: Swahili (main language)
Chigogo (one of the 150 tribal languages)

SENTENCES AND THEIR MEANINGS:
Cili waswanu du – We are well
Lyaswa – The sun has set
Lyasweza – The sun has truly set
Mbera, mbera, lete wuzeru – Quickly, bring a light
Muli waswana – Are you well?
Swanu muno muno – It is a thing of joy
Zo'sweru, Daudi – Good evening, Bwana
Zo wusweru gwe gwe – Good evening to you, Bwana

WORDS IN ALPHABETICAL ORDER:

Asante – Thank you

Askari – police officers

Bwana – name of respect

Charka – tossed in a heap

Chenga – African alarm cry

Chewi – the leopard

Chibwa – small dog

Chimate – Little Spit

Dudus – fleas

Dukas – shops

Fundi – an expert

Gramophoni – record player

Hodi? – May I enter?

Ilimba – musical instrument

Kabisa – completely

Karibu – Come in

Kenda – nine

Kisu - hunting knife

Knobkerrie – knobbed stick

Kumi – ten

Kumi na moja – eleven

Kwaheri – goodbye

Lulu baha – straight away

Mahala matitu – Black magic

Malenga – water

Masiafu – ants

Matumbiko – sacrifices

Mbwuka – good day

Nane – eight

Ndio, Bwana – Yes, sir

Ng'o – no

Pani – flea

Panya – rat

Saba – seven

Sikuku - celebration day

Singila – musical instrument

Tabu sana – great trouble

Twa – full to the neck

Wahindi – Indian shopkeepers

Wazee – the elders

Mapepo – evil spirits

Matama – corn

Mbukwenyi – greetings

Muzinzi – sweet

Nani – who

Nhembo – elephant

Nzoka-mbaha – python

Panga – knife

Pumba – bran

Shauri – discussion

Simba – lion

Sukari guru – brown sugar lumps

Tuwi – Owl

Viswanu – right/good

Watu wote – everybody

Wuvimbo – swollen places

Fact File: Characters

Let's find out about the people in the story before we start. Bwana is the Chief Doctor and the one telling the stories. Daudi is his assistant. Take a moment or two now to familiarise yourself with the names of the people you will meet in this book.

Bwana – Chief Doctor

Chibwa – the small dog

Chimate/Kisu – Chibwa's owner

Daudi – Doctor's deputee

Elisha – carpenter

Mboga (Spinach) – hospital worker

M'temi – the high chief

Mzito – Mboga's wife

Palata – a thief

Perisi – nurse, wife of Simba

Pumba – the witchdoctor

Sechelela – head nurse

Simba – Lion hunter

Suliman – the Indian

Sumbili – the chief

1
Invitation to the Feast

'Bwana, doctor, they're delicious roasted!'

Five heads nodded.

'Will you come and eat with us, Bwana?'

'Truly, Great One, it's a *sikuku* of great merit.'

Another voice chimed in. 'There is no meat as sweet to the palate as that of Panya.'

Out of the corner of my mouth I asked my African assistant. 'As the meat of what, Daudi?'

'Panya, the rat, Bwana,' he murmured, barely moving his mouth but rolling his eyes understandingly.

Louder he said, 'In the days of initiation into the tribe there is no greater delicacy than the roasted flesh of Panya.'

I turned to the boys. 'This is an invitation of great kindness but I would not rob you of your feast.'

A chorus of answers came:

'*Ng'o*, Bwana, there is plenty for all.'

'We caught a great heap of them.'

'There are eighty-seven, Bwana.'

'It would bring joy to your stomach.'

'Truly, they're delicious roasted.'

It was hard to keep a straight face.

'*Yoh*, behold it's a thing of sadness to me that the flesh of Panya, the rat, brings little joy to my stomach. Rather than reduce the size of your feast, let me add to it with another bringer of happiness.'

'*Sukari guru*,' came a voice, and they trooped off as Daudi picked up a saw and, in the room where we made medicines, cut a great block of brown, sticky, crude sugar into hunks the size of a closed fist. He picked up one of these, turned it over and prised out a cockroach which he flicked contemptuously aside.

'Eighty-seven rats is good hunting, Bwana. There is no shortness of food. Are you sure you will not come?'

I was sure.

At that moment, south of my ribs, I felt a fear growing that all was not well in the plains of Tanzania. Apparently I showed it for Daudi raised his eyebrows. 'Bwana, you feel that way too? It is well that Simba, the hunter, is with us.'

'*Eheh*, there is danger in the air – or at least something that smells like it. There must be thousands of rats about.'

'Truly, but that is because of the rainy season and the growth of the corn. There is food all over the place.'

As he spoke a hawk swooped down on the peanut garden and was in the air again in a second, clutching a rat in its talons.

That evening the ominous voice was still loud within me. There were some clues that needed careful sifting. I took a book from the shelf, started to read the latest medical information on tropical disease and made page after page of notes. From outside came some loud yelling and from the cornstalk hut where Simba's initiation boys were camped echoed shouts of delight. Daudi came to the door to give me the night report of the hospital.

'*Zo'sweru*, Daudi – good evening, Bwana.'

'*Zo wusweru gwe gwe* – good evening to you, Bwana.'

'What's all the excitement?'

'*Koh*, these are big days in the life of an African boy, Bwana, these days of initiation. Listen. Simba teaches them special things. They rub their bodies with white pipe clay and they have a deep feeling of considerable importance within them. Are they not leaving childhood and becoming members of the tribe?'

'They may have joy, Daudi, but I have a hollow feeling as though something ugly is about to happen. I don't know what it is, but I'm convinced that it's my responsibility to stop it. If this vague threat isn't traced and stamped out, there could be terrible trouble.'

Daudi nodded. 'I too have this feeling inside me and it gives me no joy.'

I agreed. 'Perhaps the biggest thing that Christians can share is talking with God.'

Again Daudi nodded. Together we knelt and told God about it, asking for his wisdom and for keen minds to cope with any situation that might arise.

As Daudi walked back to the hospital, I settled down to read a chapter from the Bible, but I did not absorb much of it. It was about the Philistines fighting with Israel, but it did not seem to have any bearing on the problem. Rather abruptly I closed the book and prepared to go to bed.

Simba and his charges were still sitting round the fire outside their hut. He had obviously been telling them a story, for little gusts of laughter came on the evening air, followed by quiet singing. He was not only teaching them the ways of the tribe, but introducing them to the ways of the kingdom of God.

As I tucked in the mosquito net there was nothing to be heard outside but the voices of crickets.

It was a hot, windless night. I tossed about, thinking of this and that and planning the next day's operations. At long last came drowsiness, brushed suddenly out of the way by the grunting of a lion.

Shouting came from Simba's cabin. '*Mbera, mbera, lete wuzeru* – quickly, bring a light!'

A handful of grass was thrown on the embers of

the fire. The blaze showed up a large tawny-maned lion between the camp and the hospital. More grass was heaped on the fire and a hundred anxious eyes watched the great beast walk slowly back through a gap in the thornbush.

For the next hour his grunting and roaring could be heard. For me, sleep had disappeared. I lit the lamp and tried to work out a chess problem, but a procession of African creatures kept moving through my thoughts. Strangely enough, none of them was a lion.

'*Hodi?*' came a voice at the door, speaking in Swahili. 'May I enter?'

'*Karibu*, Simba. Come in.'

The broad-shouldered hunter entered.

'We seem to have visitors tonight.'

'*Eheh*, Bwana. Make no mistake, he will return. Not tonight, but some other time. I have examined his footprints carefully. He is a lion that limps – an old one. He no longer hunts buck and wildebeest and zebra. He goes for less nimble game.'

'Like you and me.'

Simba grinned. 'And the children, Bwana. What are we going to do about it?'

'There is my old rifle.' I pointed to an ancient .22, a most inaccurate firearm. 'But that would not even bend his skin!'

'*Eheh*, and if you wound a lion his rage is great. Lions are shy in the daytime, but at night they have no fear.'

'Did you not kill a lion once with a spear?'

'Truly, Bwana, but it is the sort of thing that you

have no desire to do twice. I have had thoughts.'

'Have you? So have I. Nothing but thoughts all night long.'

Simba grinned again. 'Is it that lions scare you?'

'They do, but that isn't what scares me most. There is something vague and threatening that I can feel but I don't understand yet.'

'Bwana, let us then first deal with the lion.'

'*Viswanu* – right. What are your ideas?'

'I have arrows. I can shoot and not miss.'

'*Yoh*, but if you do, or if you merely wound?'

'Bwana, I will not miss but probably I will only wound. This is where I want your help. The lion must die quickly or people will. What I need is a poisoned arrow, one tipped with poison of strength.'

'We have what you want in my special cupboard with the skull and crossbones on it. But surely this is more a task for a medicine man than for me?'

The hunter grinned. 'We want to kill with certainty and speed, Bwana.'

I unlocked the poison cupboard. From a blue bottle I poured some white powder and took a dozen small pills from a glass phial. I ground these into a fine powder and mixed the lot into a paste with lanoline.

Simba went to the door and came back with his bow and three arrows. Carefully this deadly ointment was smeared over the barb of each arrow.

'Watch that stuff. It's a mixture of two powerful poisons, strychnine and cyanide. If any of your hunters were to get some of that into them it would be the end – and quickly.'

Simba nodded. 'I will guard those arrows with care. Listen, Bwana.'

From further out in the thornbush came the roar of a lion. '*Hongo*, the walls of his stomach kiss each other, and he has no joy.'

'You think he will not return tonight, but the hearts of many people will beat more quickly than usual because of tonight's happenings?'

'*Ngheeh*, Bwana, and many will place outside their houses the special medicine they think keeps lions from entering. Behold, it is a good night for witchdoctors and darkness and creatures that slink.' Simba spat. 'Can you not feel that tonight is a night of fear and danger?'

2
A Lion by Night

There was a tenseness about the hospital that day. Everyone had been talking about the lame lion. Simba had the whole initiation camp practising with spears and bows and arrows. He had placed worthless small melons on the top of a post and the archers stood thirty paces away.

From the dispensary window I watched arrow after arrow fly harmlessly past the target. Then three times in succession a melon leapt into the air, transfixed.

Daudi's smile was broad. 'Bwana, those are Simba's shots. *Yoh*, he's a *fundi*, an expert. He is sudden death to melons!'

'*Eheh*, I only hope he can shoot as well in the dark as he can in the daylight. He will have something with more teeth and claws than a melon to shoot tonight.'

Daudi nodded. 'The children have again killed many rats, Bwana.'

'*Koh*! Lions don't eat rats.'

'Truly, but it is the smell of blood and of meat that attracts. Also, Bwana, today they kill a goat for a feast, and Simba is carefully making sure that if the lion comes, it will come towards the initiation camp.'

In the middle of the morning Mboga brought me a cup of tea. 'There is news from the hills to the east. It seems that death in a strange form is found over there. Of course, there is much talk of spells and witchcraft.'

'Will you find out all you can about it, Mboga?'

I looked out through the window. A score of hovering vultures gave me an acute awareness of danger.

Two men were talking as they went past.

'*Yoh*,' said one, 'did you see Tuwi - the Owl, in the buyu tree at the hospital? Truly the ancestors have no joy in the place these days.'

I put my head through the window. '*Heh*, it is because Tuwi, the owl, has joy in eating small rats that he is about in the daytime.'

They looked at me and shrugged. 'Bwana, when you know as much about Tuwi as we do, you will not say things like that.' They walked on.

Sechelela, the African head nurse, came past.

'Well, Grandmother, your bones always ache when there is trouble in the air.'

She looked at me and shook her head. 'Bwana, you joke?'

'*Uhuh*, not really, Sech. I am uncomfortable inside.'

'*Eheh*,' she nodded. 'It is a real feeling. *Hongo*, these last two days my bones have indeed brought me no joy.'

For the next two hours her bones and my apprehensions were forgotten as I operated.

Daudi and I were scrubbing our hands. '*Yoh*, doctor!' He smiled. 'Two hours work and two lives are saved. Surely there is much to be said for surgery.'

Thoughtfully I nodded. 'Yes, while your hand works you forget everything else, but even now that voice is muttering inside me.'

'*Koh*,' broke in Mboga, 'I know, Bwana, the voice that says, "Behold, there is famine within!"'

'You're right. I certainly could do with a little dinner.'

'If you feel hungry, doctor,' said Daudi, 'what about that lion, the old beast with the lame paw? Will not famine make him cunning and daring and dangerous?'

Mboga's face was solemn. '*Kumbe*, it would be an easy thing for a lion to leap through the window of the doctor's house. Mosquito wire surely is no great obstacle to a hungry lion. It is a good thing that your wife and children are away, Bwana.'

I turned to Daudi and said in English, 'He's a happy little bunch of spinach, that Mboga.'

Daudi didn't smile but replied in the same language, 'Doctor, he is a scared bunch of spinach and so are many of us. All day long rumours have come. There are drums beating, drums you can scarcely hear. The skin creeps on many bones, eyes are wider opened and ears are used more carefully than they have been for many, many days.'

As I sat down to my meal, drums started to beat.

Right through the afternoon they beat on. I struggled with monthly reports, ushered a baby into the world and supervised the rat-proofing of our grain store. Then a nurse came running.

'Bwana, quickly! A child has swallowed a safety-pin!'

'Was it closed or open?'

'We do not know, Bwana. Quickly!'

The child was too young to be able to tell us anything about it. There was a scratch on his tongue and his lips were bleeding. He yelled at the top of his voice as I tried to look down his throat.

Then came Sechelela's calm voice. 'How many safety-pins were there in this ward?'

'Only three,' said the nurse.

'Are you sure?'

'*Eheh*, I'm sure. Two are now keeping bandages in position and the third I put on the stool over there. When I came in the baby lay on the ground screaming. The stool lay legs up. The children said that he swallowed the pin. They saw him put it into his mouth.'

The nurse held a torch while I peered down the infant's throat. It was a battle to see anything.

Sechelela spoke again. 'There is indeed a pin in the bandage of each of the two children in bed and I can see the third pin against the wall beside the table.'

The child gulped as I took the depressor out of its mouth. The nurse let out a sigh of relief and a chuckle came from the old African woman.

I smiled at her. '*Yoh*, well now that's a good thing. Probably all our fears and doubts are like that.'

She shook her head most decidedly. '*Uhuh*, doctor, do not make that mistake.'

Strikingly few people were around the village as the sun set. The cattle had been driven in early. The still evening air was full of the sound of cows returning.

Simba had a pile of firewood ready for the camp fire. Squatting on a three-legged stool beside him was Mboga with one of the local musical instruments, a *singila*. In the distance this looked strikingly like a hunter's bow.

The hunter came across to me. 'Bwana, I have no doubt that the lame lion will come tonight.'

Mboga had struck up a tune on his *singila* and it went on endlessly like a dirge.

Simba kept time with his foot for a while and then said, 'My strong ones are ready for work tonight. Each has his axe and his spear.'

'I only hope they don't get in the way if anything does happen.'

'Bwana, I have given them instructions this afternoon.'

Simba put his hand on my shoulder, bowed his head and said, 'Almighty God, help us tonight. Give us clear heads and strong hands that we may prove ourselves worthy members of your family.'

I breathed an 'Amen' and watched the muscular hunter walk unhurriedly across to his camp fire.

Mboga's *singila* went on and on that evening. Sometimes he sang, minstrel-fashion, the stories of Africa long ago, sometimes he told the adventures of great chiefs and hunters. The moon was at the quarter and night quite vague as far as light was concerned. Standing in the shadow I could see Simba, alert.

The boys were singing the initiation songs. They swayed as they sang, their closely shaven heads moving rhythmically to and fro like targets at a shooting gallery. They stood out clearly against the pale light of the horizon. There was a clearing fifty metres wide between me and the glow of their camp fire.

Into this pool of darkness came a vague, stealthy movement. Simba moved suddenly. There was a twang and a deep roar.

I pressed the button of a powerful torch. The white beam focused on a large lion squatting on its haunches, its teeth bared. It turned in the direction of the light and made as if to spring. Then suddenly it fell back, its paws twitching.

Simba's voice came with authority through the darkness. 'Everybody stand well away. Bwana, keep the light on.'

He moved steadily forward. I saw him leap and plunge his spear into the heaving chest of the great beast.

The night was quickly full of sounds of drums and of women trilling with their tongues in triumph. Everybody was crowding round the dead animal. Simba's boys looked as though each had been personally responsible for its slaughter.

One boy carefully stretched out the tail and then measured the great animal. His voice came loudly, 'It is a large lion.'

There was much laughter, very relieved laughter.

Simba whispered to me, 'Bwana, that medicine had strength, truly.'

'*Eheh*, and the aim of the arrow wasn't too bad either.'

Simba spoke quietly, 'The strong hand of God was on mine.'

A voice from behind us said, 'Bwana!'

It was Daudi. He led me a little away from the

group. 'A message has come. Three people have died and seven others are ill. They all come from the same village – away over there.' He pointed to the distant hills in the moonlight. 'The people say it is witchcraft, but doctor, you and I know better.'

'*Kumbe*, Sechelela's bones do not ache for nothing.'

3
The Puzzle of Panya

'Those puzzles, doctor – little pieces of wood, cut, twisted, with many strange arms and legs…'

'Jigsaw puzzles, Daudi. What of them?'

'This ugly feeling we have, these rumours we hear… are they not jigsaw bits?'

'They are, but they're all tossed in a heap – *charka*, as we say in Chigogo.'

He smiled. 'In English you say *higgle piggle*?'

'Something rather like that. You can see little bits of the picture, enough to make it most interesting but not enough to know what it's all about. We need more pieces, Daudi, and more of them fitting together.'

'*Ngheeh*, doctor,' he replied, 'and what do we do now?'

'There's only one way to know the truth of a rumour. We must go and see exactly what's happening.'

'I agree. Let us go *lulu baha* – straight away.'

29

'*Lulu baha* it is,' I repeated. 'Let's call Simba and Mboga. We'll leave quietly in an hour.'

Over by the initiation camp there was considerable singing and drumming, which was sufficient to cover the sound of our departure as we drove down the hill towards the village where death had struck so suddenly.

Again and again the headlights showed rats scampering across the track. Jackals seemed to be everywhere. The road wound downhill and across a dry riverbed. A squat figure stood in the centre of the track, his hand raised. With brakes screaming I pulled up.

'*Hongo,*' cried Mboga, 'it's Elisha, the carpenter.'

He stood on the running board. '*Mbwuka*, Bwana – good day.'

'*Mbwuka*, Elisha.'

'What's up?' called Daudi.

The carpenter rolled his eyes and muttered in Swahili, '*Tabu sana* – great trouble. Do not go near the village of Matama. It is a place of death.'

'*Hongo*, tell us more.'

'People have a strong sickness there.' He held up both hands. 'Ten are already dead.'

'We're on our way there now, Elisha. Where there is disease and death we must go and fight it.'

The carpenter pushed the fez back on his head and spat. 'There is no profit in going there now. Pumba, the witchdoctor, is searching for the cause of the trouble. He and the chief, Sumbili, have small joy in each other and the story is that strong death medicine made from the burnt heart of a deadly snake has been placed in the food of Pumba's family. Already five of them have died.'

'*Heeh*!' Simba broke in, 'this is trouble talk indeed.'

'*Ngheeh*, and now suddenly Sumbili has the sneezing disease. *Yoh*, he is a *fundi* at sneezing, even rivalling the Bwana here.'

'*Kah*! The sneezing disease, hay fever, is not produced by spells but by pollen from grasses!'

31

'But, Bwana, this sneezing comes suddenly, and spells are a convenient way of explaining that *mapepo - evil spirits*, are attacking.'

'Truly, Elisha. Get in. We'll drive on and be there soon. You can help us.'

The carpenter was suddenly agitated. 'If you go by night all your plans to help may be spoiled.'

'But if we delay, people may die.'

'Bwana, if you have not the confidence of the Chief, the delay of hours may be turned into days. Does not our proverb say that, "Hurry, hurry has no blessing?"'

'Tell us your words that we may hear the whole matter,' urged Simba.

The carpenter went into great detail. As he finished, Daudi turned to me. 'Doctor, his words are true. To go tonight would be a way of small profit.'

'What do you think, Simba?'

'*Eheh*, I agree.'

Mboga grinned. 'Even I, poor small-wisdomed Spinach, agree.' Suddenly he was serious. 'Bwana, I think we should go early in the morning, and I think also we should take more medicines than we have in the bag here. We should take a small hospital with us.'

I turned the truck slowly and we drove back the way we had come. There was still the sound of drums and singing and trilling tongues.

'Go and have some sleep. We will need all our strength tomorrow.'

Daudi hung back. When the others had moved up the track and into the darkness he said, 'Do any more small bits of puzzle fit together?'

I shook my head. 'No, Daudi, there are more bits of puzzle than we started with, but none fit together yet. Let me think the matter through tonight. Will you see that the truck is loaded so that we have bedding for fifteen beds and the medicines we should need for a week's supply in a hospital ward?'

Daudi nodded. 'Also syringes and needles and some instruments and the sterilizer.'

It was my turn to nod and then bid him, '*Kwaheri* – goodbye.'

For a long time I peered through the mosquito wire of my window towards the stricken village of Matama. With a sigh I idly picked up a copy of the East African Standard. At the bottom of a column in small print was an item which I carefully cut out. Here was a whole handful of jigsaw clues.

The hands of my watch pointed to midnight. Carefully I went over Elisha's story point by point.

- The Chief is hostile to the witchdoctor.
- Vicious spells are believed cast.
- There is a whispered story of medicines sprinkled in a magic circle around the Chief's house.
- The rumour of snake's heart burnt, powdered and put into witchdoctor's food.
- The plague of rats.
- A dozen unexplained deaths.
- That odd word Elisha had used – *Wuvimbo*. It could only mean 'swollen places', not boils, carbuncles or abscesses.

- The strange story about that old reprobate Palata having a pocketful of money – Palata, who would eat anything and steal the most useless and repulsive things.

- And last, but highly important, the clipping from the newspaper.

On my knees I thanked God for the help given in the matter of the lion and I prayed for wisdom in solving the puzzle of Matama and coping with it. Then I tucked in the mosquito net and tried to sleep.

The drums beat on monotonously. They throbbed in my head like an aching tooth. Over and over in my mind turned the pieces of the puzzle. Death, old Palata, and a cascade of rats.

Then I heard a mosquito in the net. Leaving that insect alive could mean malaria. I sat up and shone a light around. Down the beam it flew. Smack! No more mosquito.

I lay back and thought of lions and mosquitoes. How much more dangerous mosquitoes were and how little they worried people, while a lion could terrify a whole village.

The pillow seemed hard. I shook it and underneath was my Bible. I switched on the torch and started to read a bit more about the Philistines in 1 Samuel. Israel was in trouble for the age-old reason – they had turned their backs on God. The Philistines were warriors. How they must have had their tails up when they captured the ark of God.

I read on but the words didn't sink in. That wretched

throbbing drum! I would have liked to take it and dump it over the head of the drummer and use his sticks with vigour where they would do him most good.

Then I started counting sheep. It was useless. Lions kept coming into the picture, and rats, piles of them.

Over went my thoughts to the ark of God. What was in it? Aaron's rod that budded, the pot of manna, the stones with the Ten Commandments on them.

I started to recite the commandments, but only reached the second when my thoughts flew off to graven images – the Fish God Dagon that I had been reading about, and then 'tumours'. The Philistines had been attacked by some sort of disease in epidemic form and had developed tumours, swellings. What were they?

Tumours and mice!

Mice! Mice! What was this?

The drummer was still at it.

Bother the drummer!

Mice and tumours.

There was a commentary on my desk. Things were taking shape, but the pieces still didn't quite fit.

Out of bed I swung and lighted a hurricane lantern. There was a moderate-sized scorpion not far from my foot. Hostile brutes, scorpions. He really shaped up as a slipper came into accurate action.

I scooped the corpse up on a newspaper and put it in the waste-paper basket, and turned over the pages of the Bible commentary and read for a while. Then I turned over the pages of the Old Testament to 1 Samuel 15 and read again.

In my mind the whole puzzle fell into place. Bubonic plague!

The puzzle was solved. At last I knew what we were fighting. That drummer was still at it. He could drum till dawn for all I cared now.

Quietly I prayed again. The pattern of things was now clear, but the way to cope with it was quite another matter.

Sleep came quickly. My next conscious thought was to answer a voice which called '*Hodi!*' at the window.

'*Karibu* – come in,' I answered sleepily.

'Dawn in about twenty minutes, doctor,' came Daudi's voice.

Before we set out, we stood with heads bowed around old Sukuma, the car, and asked Almighty God to help us in a task which could mean a thousand lives saved.

Carefully I explained the details of the disease we were about to fight. There was a quiet nodding of heads as we swung on our journey. The truck slowed down to cross a particularly wide dry riverbed.

'Would any of you like to turn back?'

Daudi grinned. Elisha shook his head. Simba said, 'We will all be in this, Bwana.'

'Even I,' said Mboga cheerfully, 'may be useful.'

'You may be bitten, Vegetable.'

'So may you, Bwana. But tell me, have you heard the song about the woodcutters and the lion?'

He started and the others joined in. The road forked. 'Which way now?'

Elisha's voice directed, 'The track through the boulders to the east.'

We drove past a fantastic pile of granite that looked like a careless giant's efforts, with great, grey blocks. Then we wound up over soil-erosion-scarred shale and through a winding, just-wide-enough track between towering cactus.

'We can only go another kilometre, Bwana, and then the road is covered with boulders. We'll have to carry everything from then on.'

The soil looked better. There was grass, that tufty shivery grass that looks wonderful when blown by the wind. We unloaded, shouldered the loads, and started out in single file.

'*Yoh*!' laughed Daudi, 'this country is food for the eyes.'

'Truly, but that grass is not food for my nose. As surely as sunrise that will make me...will make me...' I dumped down my load, 'Will make me...SNEEZE!!'

4
Sneezes for Two

Ahead the thornbush and cactus-covered hills looked peaceful and tranquil. We walked up the winding single-track path, well aware that at the end of it lurked danger and death.

The track started to flatten out. The soil looked better. Simba ran some of it through his toes. '*Yoh*, Bwana, that's good earth! They grow corn in this village that is *muzinzi* — sweet!'

'That's why they call the place *Matama*, corn,' came Daudi's voice from in front.

'*Eeh*, that's why the witchdoctor has the name *Pumba*, bran,' broke in Mboga.

I stopped. '*Yoh*, Spinach, I have thought of a special task that only one of skill can perform.'

Mboga grinned. 'Here is work that has prickles in it. I, poor Vegetable, must go into places of difficulty and danger to…'

Simba broke in. 'Less babble, Spinach…Bwana, what are your thoughts?'

'That he should go to the village of Handali, spend some shillings on food and sugar, sit under the buyu tree in the marketplace before the *dukas*—shops— and talk words that will make other tongues move. In this way we will hear if any danger or cause of trouble comes from Handali. Especially, though, listen to the words of the *Wahindi* - the Indian shopkeepers, for my bones tell me…'

'When the Bwana's bones speak, these things happen,' grinned Mboga. 'The framework within him whispers wisdom almost to be compared with that produced by the bones of old Sechelela.'

I fished out some East African shillings and put them into his palm. 'Talk with purpose. Your tongue and your ears and your memory may well save lives.'

Simba stopped. 'We need the help of God, Bwana.'

'Truly, then let's ask for it.'

We bowed our heads as Simba prayed, 'Our all-capable Father, we need help greatly. Unstop our ears, hold the strings of our tongues and keep the movements of our feet. We attempt work for you, our Father and God. We are the spears and arrows in your hand. Keep us from making mistakes.'

At the end of that prayer a sudden thought struck me. I wrote a note to M'temi, the head Chief of the country.

'Deliver this yourself to no-one but the Chief. See that it goes from your hand to his.'

Mboga nodded as he bent down to pick up a stick. 'The words in the letter must be of great importance, Bwana.'

'They are, Spinach.'

He split the stick, put the folded paper into it and saying '*Kwaheri* — Goodbye' began to walk in the direction of the Chief's village.

Daudi shouldered his load and said, 'Truly the grass that grows on this hillside is food for the eyes as it bends to the wind.'

'*Naugh*! But it isn't food for my nose. When I come near that grass, behold, before you can say…can say…*atishoo*!'

Sneeze followed sneeze. My eyes and nose ran.

'Hay fever brings small joy to the Bwana,' explained Daudi.

'Your words have truth,' I gasped. With every sneeze my chest started to become tighter. It became increasingly hard to speak. I held up my hand and panted, 'Slower—men. The invisible—bands that—grip my chest—are tightening and—when they tighten there—is no chance of walking—with speed.'

'It is the disease called asthma,' remarked Daudi.

'A complaint of small comfort,' replied Simba politely.

'It's a—jolly pest,' I gulped.

At a reduced pace we climbed the slope. Ahead were the huts of the village. In front of the Chief's place were a crowd of people.

With every step speech became more difficult. At last we stood before the Chief and a crowd of a hundred people. They were unsmiling.

'*Mbukwenyi*,' said the Chief, and sneezed.

I sneezed also and greeted, '*Mbukwenyi*.'

'*Muli waswana*—are you well?' asked the Chief. His eyes were red and he sniffed ineffectively to cope with a running nose. He was obviously finding it hard to breathe.

'*Cili waswanu du*—we are well,' I replied. My voice seemed to mimic his. There was a sudden hostile whispering.

The Chief sneezed.

I sneezed.

He came unsteadily to his feet. 'It is no—matter for laughter—this trouble!'

I sneezed and sneezed again.

The Chief shook his fist. 'I, Sumbili, have anger. Why should you—mock me?'

My own breathing was so difficult now that I panted out, 'I do not—mock, Great One. I suffer—too! Can —

a person sneeze at will? Do eyes run at— their owner's bidding? Does anyone rejoice—to have—tight bands around—his—chest?'

Sumbili leaned towards me, his attitude changed. '*Yoh*, Bwana, I—did not understand.'

We both sneezed at the same time, and laughing huskily we gripped hands. He ordered a stool to be brought for me. We sat sneezing, panting, and having a session of mutual pity.

'There is—much strength in- this-disease, Bwana!'

'Truly, and—small joy. Do you feel that to breathe is—a matter of great—importance—and considerable difficulty?'

'*Eheeeh*! It is as—though *Nzoka-mbaha*—the python, were coiled—about your ribs.'

'Exactly, and—he tightens his—coils.'

'It is a thing—of small comfort, truly. Often I feel—that rawhide is—around my shoulders and—it contracts. *Eeeeh*!'

I explained about allergy and how it worked. The Chief looked at me with incredulity in his eyes. I spoke softly so that only he could hear.

'I know the news—of the—village. The secret words—that magic and strong medicine has—been placed around your—house. Believe me, O Sumbili, the—cause of your trouble—is tiny things in—the—air. When you—see a thin shaft of—sunlight do not small things dance—in it? The pollen from—grass and—from flowers and—trees, these tickle the nose—of some and—they—sneeze. And they breathe with—great effort only. In others their—skin swells and itches,

43

their—noses, ears, eyes, irritate—beyond belief...'

I paused, panting, after the effort of so long a speech.

Sumbili nodded doubtfully. 'All this sorrow – attacks my body, but—how are we to—know the cause?'

'The words of – the books of medicine describe—it, pictures show it, the—experiences—of thousands — are written—down.'

'*Yoh*!' Sumbili raised his eyebrows.

'There was no—witchdoctor to walk around—my house in Australia, Great—One, and yet—I had the trouble—there. Everywhere through—the whole—world people suffer this way.'

I groped in my pocket, producing first a hypodermic syringe and then a small glass ampoule branded Adrenalin. A whispering commenced, but this time with no hostility in it.

'Great One, I have no—desire further to feel—these bonds about me. With your—permission, I shall—use a medicine of strength—to tear them—apart.'

Off came the top of the ampoule. I rubbed my leg with a swab of cotton wool, carefully measured the medicine and briskly injected it. The whispering was continuing. I was watched by hundreds of wary eyes.

Daudi spoke, 'The Bwana has many medicines of great power—medicines that control troubles that worry the people of our country.'

'*Yoh*,' gasped the Chief, 'the medicine does—not yet untie—his chest.'

'Does porridge cook in a moment?' retorted Daudi. 'Is an egg laid without any cackle in it?'

There was a ripple of laughter.

'*Yoh*,' spoke a wondering voice, 'see him.'

'*Ngheeh*, I breathe with greater ease. *Eheh*! It is a matter of no little relief to loose the invisible bonds that tie up your chest.'

Daudi was carefully looking at the village. He saw things which told a whole story to his nimble mind, but which meant nothing to me.

The Chief and others of his inner circle watched me extremely carefully. After about five minutes Sumbili spoke.

'Bwana, give me—also this bond—loosening—medicine. There is still some—in the bottle.'

'*Ng'o*. Suppose it were to poison you? Do I wish to feel the spears of these men of muscles?'

'Bwana, it did not—poison you. It will—not poison —me. See—there is still—half the—medicine—in the little bottle.'

'It may do you no good. If this happens you will have anger. I have no wish to give you false hopes.'

The Chief shook his head. 'It worked for—you. It will—work for me. It helped you. It will—help me.'

There was a nodding of heads and a strong under-current of whispering.

'I will give it to you, Great One, for our medicines work. We both have the same trouble. You saw it work for me. It did me no harm. Therefore you seek the same medicine for your trouble.'

Sumbili nodded. I loaded the syringe. In a moment the needle was driven home. Everyone watched the Chief. From back in the village came a noise which made Simba look up apprehensively.

He murmured, 'The witchdoctor has no joy in seeing his spell torn apart.'

The whole village was watching the Chief.

A minute passed. 'It does—not work.'

'*Yoh*! Even in this village a grain of corn planted does not become a cob in an hour,' said Daudi quickly.

There was a drum beating oddly in the background with a sense of hostility in the sound.

Then the Chief stood up, a slow smile spreading over his face. 'They're loosening. It's easier. *Yoh— heeh*! That's medicine.' He stretched his arms widely. '*Hongo*, I can breathe.' He took a deep breath and grasped my hand. 'That's wonder-medicine, Bwana.'

'When you've had a trouble, O Chief, it makes a lot of difference in understanding the sorrows of others, and the cause of them.'

Nodding gravely he said, 'Truly, Bwana, we will rejoice to taste more of your medicine.'

'May we therefore camp here for a while?'

'*Ngheeeh*, Bwana. My men will help.'

Soon a track was cleared and the truck was in the village.

46

Elisha, the lame carpenter, supervised the unloading. We had a tent and a movable wooden half-shed, half-hospital, that could be put together in an hour or so.

The tent was erected in minutes. Then the movable four-bed hospital took shape at amazing speed. Bolts were fixed, beams fitted, the floor screwed into position and the roof of canvas was stretched into place.

Suddenly Simba leapt with his *knobkerrie*—knobbed stick. He seemed to be striking at a shadow, but the stick hit something with a solid whack. He turned to me.

'Panya, the rat, Bwana.' He bent down to pick it up.

'Don't touch it,' I shouted urgently. Putting on a pair of rubber gloves and taking a wide-mouthed preserving bottle from the back of the truck, I walked carefully towards the dead rat and slid it into the bottle with Simba's stick and screwed the lid on tightly.

Daudi carefully looked over the glove with a torch. 'Doctor, no *dudus* —fleas.'

'*Eheh*, just as well. It's going to be interesting to see what we find inside that bottle.'

The people were crowding round. 'Bwana, what is it all about?'

'*Yoh*,' said a hard voice, 'he is making medicine out of rats. *Heeeh*, this is evil medicine.'

'You're right. There's evil medicine in that bottle but I'm not going to make it out of a rat. Is there not a great sickness in this village?'

The Chief nodded. 'Bwana, we have great sadness. Already twelve people have died in the houses of

Matama.' He pointed with his chin to the group of flat-roofed fifty-metre long African houses which was the dwelling for a whole clan: grandparents, uncles and aunts, the whole family group.

'Great One, it is said, is it not, that medicine has been placed at the doors, that spells have been cast?'

He looked at me cautiously and then nodded. 'Bwana, these are the words.'

I held up the jar with the dead rat. 'Those that hunt in the jungle look for the paw marks of leopard and lion and buck and seeing them they say, "Animals have passed this way." In that bottle, I believe, are the footprints of this disease. The cause of death is not witchcraft. It is a disease, an evil sickness for which we have the answer.'

Simba came to my side gripping his *knobkerrie*. The crowd swayed back a little. A striking figure strode towards us—Pumba, the witchdoctor. On his wrists were large white circlets of ivory and round his neck the eye-teeth of leopards. His buffalo-skin head-dress was quivering with rage. He spoke not a word but stood there glaring.

Without warning he swung a long, ornamented knobbed stick and the jar crashed into pieces at my feet.

Simba moved forward to attack. I dragged him back.

'Forget him. He can do small harm. This dead rat is much more deadly.' The crowd backed away. 'Kerosene, Daudi, quickly.'

He pushed a lantern into my hands. I poured the oil from it over the carcass and the broken glass, struck a match, and the flames leapt up. I sighed with relief, to the amazement of the Chief.

'Bwana, why do that?'

'Bring grass and wood that the rat may be burnt to ashes. Let me prepare first, Great One, and then I will explain everything.'

5

Witchdoctor Worried

Night came suddenly. Only a few things remained to be done.

Pumba had lit a fire. He squatted on the ground outside his house with its flat mud roof and its wicker-work mud-plastered walls. Tragedy had come into this long dark African house. Three times in two days

death had struck at his family. First an old man, weak with age, then a child and, now at sundown, a young woman had made the great journey.

He beat the drum with an eerie rhythm, and an old woman with staring, vacant eyes crouched opposite him. From time to time her lips opened to emit the alarm cry.

We watched from the other side of the village. Daudi spoke softly, 'He drums out the evil spirits, doctor. *Eeeh*-see!'

Slowly an owl flew by and perched on the hut roof.

'Witchdoctors use owls for messengers.' The bird swooped to the ground and flew into the darkness, a small rat in its beak.

The scene was dimly lit by a half moon and the flickering camp fire. As the witchdoctor drummed on the woman opposite him started to twitch convulsively. The village watched in fear and fascination.

'See, doctor, behind him.' A rat staggered weakly out of the mud house and collapsed beside the drum. I took a pace forward but Simba gripped my arm.

'No, Bwana, to meddle in any way could cause great anger.'

'Not to deal with that rat could cost him his life.'

Daudi spoke quietly, 'You mustn't do it, doctor. This is a thing of the tribe. He is calling the ancestors. *Mapepo*, spirits, fill the old woman, his assistant. If we interfere we could be out out of the village with not a pill swallowed or an injection given.'

I nodded silently, but inside me a voice warned, 'The rat's fleas are the danger.'

The drumming went on and on. 'To stand there watching futilely is a thing of small profit,' I whispered. 'Let us finish our preparation.'

We fitted out the back of the truck as a rat-proof sleeping place. Medicines, microscope, sterilizer – all were set out. We checked and rechecked everything.

It was nearing midnight when the warriors outside the Chief's hut started to shout. The silhouettes of their muscular bodies against the night sky told of tension and awareness of danger.

Then came the tinkle of an *ilimba*.

'It's Mboga,' said Daudi, running forward and speaking with the Chief's men. They sat down and Mboga greeted them as he walked across to me.

'*Lyaswa* - the sun has set,' he said.

'*Lyasweza* - it is truly set,' I replied, following the formula.

'Bwana, much news. The High Chief M'temi says that he agrees and to refrain from worrying, for he comes with fast-moving feet.'

'That's splendid. And what of the doings at Handali?'

'The uncle of Suliman the Indian had arrived, and many of his cousins. They travelled from the country of India. They have small joy, for in their luggage, Panya the rat had a party and died in a way that their noses will long remember. *Yoh*, their words were strong and pointed.'

In my hand I held the cutting from the paper which first had made me aware of danger. It read, 'Severe outbreak of bubonic plague in Bombay.'

Somehow an infected rat had found its way into their clothing. It had travelled across the Indian Ocean and, although it was very dead, its fellow-criminal the flea had managed to survive.

'Palata, that rascal of a man truly called the Cockroach,' went on Mboga, 'saw a blanket hanging on a bush behind the shop of Suliman. It stank, but that was a matter of small importance to Palata. He stole it and came to this village.'

Daudi sprang to his feet and ran to the Chief's house and in a minute he was back. 'Doctor, the whole thing is clear now. Palata brought the blanket here and sold it to Pumba!'

I whistled. 'Call everyone together, Daudi. This is the full picture, but first we must do battle against our most deadly enemy, the flea.'

We bandaged over our shoes and halfway to the hips. Mboga produced the white canvas shoes he had bought at the Indian shops. He and Simba, who were bare-footed, put these on. I checked over the bandaging and stuck strips of sticking plaster to keep the narrow cloth from slipping.

'The *dudu*-gun, Elisha.'

The carpenter nodded and brought an insecticide spray. He worked hard on our legs and feet, fore and aft. The village was thoroughly awake, and everything we did was followed by hundreds of inquiring eyes.

The witchdoctor was still drumming behind the house, and it seemed only metres away, a hyaena howled.

'*Kah*,' said Elisha, 'this is a night to make coldness creep beneath your skin.'

'*Yoh*,' came Mboga's voice with a smile in it, 'wearing these bandages makes my skin hot and itchy and there is no comfort in scratching.'

'*Heeeh*!' muttered Daudi. 'Done up like this the people will think we have charm of great power. They wonder greatly!'

'No charm was ever a better barrier than this thick calico with all that flea-fighting medicine on it. Let us talk again with the Chief.'

The witchdoctor stopped his drumming suddenly and stalked off into the darkness.

Again the hyaena howled and murmurs went round. 'Pumba has become a hyaena and he goes to cast spells.'

'Pumba crouches in the darkness,' hissed Simba. '*Kah*, I'd like to…'

Daudi suddenly sprang up excitedly. 'Over there! See it?'

'See them,' said Mboga. 'Is it not a crowd of people walking one behind the other, each with a lantern?'

'They move with speed,' said Simba. 'They are men with a purpose.'

'*Eheh*, this undoubtedly is the High Chief with his police.'

'Daudi, will you stay here with Elisha to see that all goes well and that no one interferes with our preparations? Simba, Mboga and I will go to greet the Great One.'

The line of light was still nearly a kilometre away from us. As we walked down the hill towards them, the neat formation broke up and to right and left moved a group of lanterns. After a while one would stop and the others would move on.

'*Yoh*,' said Simba, 'it is a good thing. The village will soon be ringed with lanterns and each path will be guarded by *askari*. *Hongo*, Bwana, and see, towards us comes the Great One himself with some of his people.'

Soon we saw M'temi, a tall man with an unmistakable air of authority about him, walking towards us. Two paces in front of him marched an African policeman with a rifle over his shoulder and a lantern in his hand.

I greeted the Chief and shook his hand.

'Behold, Great One, your coming brings joy to my heart and safety to very many of the whole of the tribe.'

He nodded. '*Yoh*, Bwana, I knew from your letter that the matter was of great importance. *Eheeh*, truly you look as if you have not slept for days.'

'*Eheh*, and that is how things are in this village. Death stalks through the place, death which could be a terrible one.'

'*Hongo*, what are we to do, Bwana?'

'Order your men to surround the village. Nobody – man, woman or child – must go out of this place. If anyone tries to do so they must be stopped. If they resist and run for it, they must be chased and brought back with strength.'

'I understand, Bwana. Perhaps a tap on the head would keep them quiet for a while.'

'*Eheh*, if completely necessary, but instruct your *askaris* to be careful how they tap. We don't want any more sick people, especially those with fractured skulls. And tell your men if they see any rats, those rats must be killed and burnt at once.'

M'temi nodded. Briskly he gave the orders, and I was considerably relieved when I saw a cordon of African police stationed around the village.

'Great One, it would be safer for you and your men not to go near the village. Also, there would be wisdom in spraying you with the medicine that kills *dudus*.'

Mboga approached with the insect gun.

'*Hoh*,' said the Chief, 'that stuff smells.'

'Smell or no smell, it may save your life. If your nose objects to it, imagine how the noses of *dudus* feel.'

'*Hongo*, well spray me thoroughly, Bwana.'

Mboga did so, and then he set out with the Chief's own special police sergeant to spray all of those who would act as sentries round the village.

The High Chief was a man of action. 'Bwana, what shall we do first? Call the sub-chiefs so that we can talk the whole matter over and then I will tell them what to do?'

'Excellent. Behold, the orders are going to be difficult ones. At least one house in that village must be burnt down, and every rat and every flea on the whole of this hill must be killed. If not the disease will spread right through the country and thousands of people may die. And remember, Great One, this disease has well been called the Black Death.'

6
Fireside Story

'Mboga,' I whispered, pushing a *panga* into his hand. 'Keep your eye on Pumba's house. I think he's trying to run for it. He's cunning.'

'*Ndio, Bwana.* Yes, sir.' He fingered the blade of the large knife, grinned and disappeared into the darkness.

Minutes later there was angry screaming. Vague shadows swayed towards us and into the lamplight came a thoroughly scared witchdoctor. Close behind, with the *panga* against his ribs, marched Mboga.

In a parade-ground voice he barked, 'Halt!' Whether or not the witchdoctor understood the meaning of the word I don't know, but the tone was all that could be desired. Mboga stopped suddenly, made an imposing show of presenting arms and in a sergeant-major-like voice addressed the Chief and myself. 'Great Ones, this man Pumba was trying to escape from the village. He resisted and I have brought him here under arrest.'

At that moment a hyaena howled eerily. We looked across to where the noise came from and there, outlined against the horizon, was the hunchbacked scavenger of the jungle. It lifted its head and howled again.

I asked, 'Is your sergeant a *fundi*, an expert, with the rifle?'

'*Kabisa* – completely,' replied the Chief.

'May he shoot that creature? I have a reason.'

The Chief nodded. The sergeant dropped on one knee. To me it looked a most difficult shot. I watched the sturdy figure slowly squeeze the trigger. There was a tuft of flame at the end of the rifle. Pumba nearly fell over backwards with fright at the loudness of the report. We could see the hyaena. It seemed as if it had been struck with a club. It toppled over and lay still. I turned to the Chief.

'Great One, in the house of this man, Pumba, is the worst of the disease. He is, as you know, the witchdoctor of the place. He deceives people. Do they not think that the voice of the hyaena is his voice? Has he not been crouching there among the rocks letting that four-footed sneak-thief bring fear to the hearts of many?'

Pumba's mouth was set in an angry snarl, but the Chief, in a voice that had command in every tone of it, said, 'Get back to your house and drag that hyaena behind you. Leave it lying in front of your door. You, Mboga, go with him and see that this is done.'

Mboga saluted, presented arms again, and roared instructions to the prisoner. Away they went towards the village, the witchdoctor forlornly dragging the dead animal behind him. I could hear Mboga, to whom 'right' and 'light' meant exactly the same thing, shouting, 'Light, left, light.'

Another lantern was coming up the path towards us.

'*Yoh*,' said the Chief, 'I should have told you. Behind us is another of my men and the wife of Simba, Perisi. She felt that there might be work that only a woman could do so she had to come.'

A big smile spread over Simba's face. Soon Perisi was sitting down with us round the fire and I started off, '*Watu wote* – everyone, this is a disease of death. But it is even more deadly when people do not know the cause. Recently the most important thing of all has happened. We have medicines that are the answer to this plague – these pills. Also I have carefully put away some medicine for injections to be used only if the very worst happens. Sometimes this disease spreads into the lungs of people. Then, with every cough, germs can be spread widely and people breathing them in catch the disease. This would be a terrible thing indeed.'

'*Yoh*,' said the Chief, 'how does this happen, Bwana?'

I turned to Perisi. 'In that bag you were carrying on your head, was there flour?'

She nodded.

I turned to the Chief. 'Have you any snuff in the gourd I see in your pocket?'

M'temi nodded.

'Simba, would you help me by taking a handful of flour and putting it into your mouth, just letting it stay there?'

'*Yoh*,' gulped Simba, 'I know what you are going to do, Bwana. A little snuff under my nose and I will sneeze with strength.'

'That is it. I want to show people what happens to germs in your mouth that travel four or five paces when you sneeze or cough.'

Simba filled his mouth full of flour. He rolled his eyes as the Chief flipped snuff under his nose. The hunter's eyelids closed and for a moment he was particularly tense. Those watching could see the sneeze growing and then '*A-tish-oo*!' A cloud of white flour burst from his lips.

'*Yoh*,' exclaimed the Chief. 'We understand it. Bwana, this is a thing of great danger. But you have the medicines that will answer it. Tell me, how did they find the cause?'

'This is a thing of wonder. It was about a hundred years ago that scientists made this discovery and yet, in the Bible, there it was all written down for those with open eyes and open minds to understand – written over four thousand years ago.'

'*Koh*,' said M'temi, 'tell us about it, Bwana.'

'It was the time before the days of King David. The Wafilisti, a fierce tribe, lived near the sea coast and were fishermen. Behold, they fought against the men of Israel. They were men of strength and they threw their spears expertly, and used their swords with skill. In the battles the Waisraeli were soundly beaten. Many of them were killed – very many of them, for they had made a terrible mistake. They had given up obeying God and were going the way of sin.'

'*Koh*' said Daudi, 'Bwana, have we not learned these days that the way of sin is the way of death?'

'It always happens that way. In that battle alone, four thousand of the people of Israel died. Their leaders realised that the trouble was so acute that they sent for the ark of God, which was a great box covered with gold – very beautiful indeed. In it were three things: a stick which had been used to do miracles in the land of Egypt, the Ten Commandments written on big stones, and a little box with manna, which was special bread God gave to the people of Israel when they came out of Egypt. Above the ark were two figures of angels with spread wings made all of gold.'

'*Hongo*,' said M'temi, 'Bwana, it must have been wonderful to look at.'

'It was. These people said, "We will take the ark of God and bring it, and then we will win the victory." In this way they made another mistake. It wasn't the ark alone that they needed, for beautiful as it was, it was only a reminder of God's presence with them. They didn't need the reminder, for it was God himself who could bring them the victory if only he were with them. But unless they turned their backs on sin and the ways of the devil, God wouldn't be there. They were not long in finding out their second mistake, for the Wafilisti fought like men possessed and conquered the people of Israel and captured the ark of God.

'"*Heh*," they shouted, "behold, the God of Israel is not powerful. Behold, the magic of Dagon, our god, is mightier than his."'

'Bwana,' questioned the Chief, 'what did he look like, this Dagon?'

'He was a stone image of a man carrying a large fish on his back. *Kumbe*! Behold, the priests of Dagon carried the ark of God and put it in their temple and boasted, "Our god is much greater and stronger than Jehovah, the God of the Israelites. We have seen proof of this thing in today's battle."

'So the sun set with the carved idol Dagon at one end of the temple and the ark of God in front of it.'

'Night fell, and dark corners of that temple became like the darkness and the blackness of the worship that was carried out there. They did very vile things.'

'*Koh*,' muttered Simba, 'we know this thing too. Have we not *matumbiko* - sacrifices, in our tribal worship and magic? Bwana, it can be an evil thing.'

He drew closer to the fire gripping his spear. There was an uncomfortable silence, and then M'temi said, 'Bwana, what happened?'

'While the priests of Dagon feasted and drank that night, inside the temple something special had happened. With dawn the priests came to the temple to sing their praises to their god. They had heard nothing through the darkness and didn't imagine that anything could be wrong. From the outside everything was normal. The early rays of the sun shone on the temple as usual.

'They opened the door and stood there gasping with amazement. Dagon, their great god, had fallen on his face on the ground before the ark. *Kumbe*, how those priests worked to lift the mighty image back into position! Nobody must know what had happened. All day long their minds were in a turmoil.

'How had it happened? Had some traitor climbed in and levered the great image over? It was too big for that to be done unless a whole band of men had been at work. What was behind it all?

'That night they locked the door and set a guard. Inside in the darkness, Dagon again faced the ark. They heard no sound during the night, but with the dawning the door was thrown open. Again the great image was fallen flat on the ground. Their fear was made greater when they saw that this time his head and his hands lay cut off as though an executioner had done it. Only the stump of Dagon was left. *Yoh*! Fear now mingled with their amazement. This could not be the work of men.'

I paused for a moment. There was silence from those that listened, but from the hill, in the village of Matama, came the high-pitched cry of anguish that told of death. Those who crouched around the fire shivered.

7

Declaration of War

'The Philistines had fear and with reason. The Bible tells us that the hand of God himself was as heavy upon that people as it had been upon their idol.

'Scores of them died from a great sickness. There were tumours, swellings – the same sort that we have seen in the village up there.' I pointed with my chin. 'It was the same disease, plague, and it spread through their towns and villages. The tribesmen said, "Surely this has happened because this ark is in our country."

'All their chiefs met. There was a great *shauri* and much discussion. Some said, "Send it back to the land of Israel. It may be that this evil sickness will leave us then."

'But there were those who said, "It is very valuable. There is much gold. Let us send it to another town and test whether it is really the cause of the trouble." They did this, but the plague broke out there also.

'Alarm spread among the Philistines and they said, "Let us send it back to the Israelites with a gift to appease their God." The *Wazee* - the elders of the tribe, said, "Behold, does not our land swarm with rats? Shall we not send an offering of a golden rat for each chief and five golden tumours shaped like the swellings which are the curse of this evil disease? Behold, if we do this perhaps the hand of their God will be lightened against us."

'This is what they did, and there was no more plague among the Philistines.'

'*Hongo*,' exclaimed Simba, 'can't you see it, Bwana? Lots of rats, lots of tumours.'

'Yes, that's the danger here and now. We must stop this deadly sickness from spreading.'

On the night air came the *chenga* - the African alarm cry.

'*Yoh*!' burst out Daudi. 'Doctor, this is no time for words. We must have action. Even now a new day dawns.'

There was colour in the clouds to the east.

'I agree, Daudi, and this is how I see the situation. With the help of the Chief and his *askaris*, we can have the village blocked off. Nobody can get out, nobody can come in unless...' I looked across at M'temi and asked the question by raising my eyebrows.

'Unless I say so?' Without hesitation he nodded.

'Within that village we will hunt the rats and kill them with a great slaughter. We will spray every house with medicine that kills fleas. Thus we will blunt the teeth and claws of this disease. At the same time we will treat those who are sick. The earlier they are given medicine, the quicker and more certain is the cure.

'And at all times we must be prepared for trouble to come from the house of Pumba.'

Simba nodded vigorously and turned to the Chief, who had been joined by the Headman of that village. 'Most of the people in this part of the country fear Pumba greatly. There is only one person in the whole place who is not frightened of him, and that is the Bwana, who is not a man of Africa. In many ways he's one of us, but he is not born with this fear woven into his thoughts.'

There was a pause and Simba went on, 'Great Ones, give the Bwana authority to do what he thinks is best, and M'temi strengthen the hand of Sumbili with your orders so that when he instructs the men of the village it may be known that his words are your words.'

I could see Perisi looking at her husband with eyes that glistened. She and I both realised that he was doing a very hard thing in a very wise way.

M'temi was a real leader. He leant towards me and said quietly, 'You tell Sumbili what you want done and I will order those of the village to do exactly what he says.'

'Thank you, Great One. It would be good if people hear the words from his lips.'

So it was agreed. We said *Kwaheri* to M'temi, but before going back to the village as the sun rose I prayed, 'Almighty God, help us in this battle against the disease of the body and help us to understand more clearly about the disease of the soul and its cure.'

I gripped M'temi's hand. 'Thank you. Cause your people to kill every rat they can. Rats are the danger, and the fleas that feed upon them.'

A slow smile spread over his face. 'Bwana, the tribe of Panya, the rat, will have small joy in the days that lie ahead.'

As we went back to the plague-ridden village I spoke with Sumbili. 'Let us call the people together and talk with them for a little while now, and then more fully this evening.'

Sumbili stopped. His hand was on his chest. 'Bwana, do you feel the tightness round your chest that comes from the disease that you and I suffer from particularly?'

I nodded and put a pill into his hand and swallowed one myself. 'Whenever you feel that strong cord about your chest, tell me and I will give you one of these.'

'Bwana, this is true medicine.' He stretched and breathed deeply and gave a brisk order. At once a drum started to throb and people hurried towards us. There was fear on every face. At the far end of the village I could see Mboga standing on guard outside the witchdoctor's house.

Sumbili stood up, leaning on his spear. 'As you know, M'temi, the king of our country, visited us during the night. His policemen have surrounded the village with instructions that no one should attempt to leave. If they do, they will be brought back with strength. There is a special reason for this. The Bwana here will tell you.'

I spoke. 'Chief Sumbili, and people of this hill called Matama, ugly trouble has come into your village. Two nights ago Simba here killed a lion with an arrow and a spear. People near our hospital were gripped by fear and then great relief. But today this village in which you live is surrounded by creatures more dangerous than lions, more deadly, more subtle and much more numerous.'

An uneasy murmur went around those who crowded near us. 'Over ten generations ago in England, in the great city of London, to house after house came death. This sickness they called the Great Plague. Thousands upon thousands of people died, and then came a vast fire. Half of the city was burnt to the ground, but the plague disease disappeared.

'What caused the trouble, you ask? A spell? The anger of the ancestors? The powerful magic of many witchdoctors?

'No, the answer was the sinister creatures that are here by the thousand in your own village. Let me show you this and prove it to you that your eyes may see and your minds understand.'

From Mboga came a piercing yell. Everyone turned and watched as he raced after a rat. His spear flashed and the creature was transfixed by the blade.

'Bring it over here, Mboga, on the very end of your spear.' He did so, holding it well away from his body. 'And, Daudi, fetch that tin of honey. Elisha, bring that kerosene tin you flattened out.'

A minute later, squatting in front of the crowd, Daudi smeared honey thickly over the square of tin.

'Put the rat down carefully in the middle of the honey, Mboga.'

'Watch, everybody, then you will understand the reason for today's special work. No flea can jump further than the span of a man's hand. It is not the habit of fleas to stay on dead rats. Watch, and see them leap off. Their feet will become entangled in the honey and then we will examine them.'

Simba's voice was tense. 'There goes one, Bwana, see.' The flea had leapt into the honey. It struggled and then sank stickily. 'There's another, Bwana, and another and another.'

'Mboga, light the primus stove and put a pot of water on it.' When the water was boiling I put on long rubber gloves, picked up the rat gingerly by the tail and dipped it into the boiling water.

'*Yoh*, what is he doing?' came a chorus of whispers.

I looked up. 'No flea has joy in boiling water. Do this and there is no risk of being bitten by one of those death-carrying *dudus*.'

The next step was to dissect the rat. It was obviously riddled with plague. To the Chief and those who stood around I pointed out the damage done by the disease. They nodded their heads understandingly. Then I took a swollen lymph gland and smeared it on a glass slide. Everybody watched spellbound as it was stained with various dyes and dried. Then one of the fleas was lifted out of the honey, crushed between two glass slides, and stained.

We put the microscope out on a box. I picked up a large textbook on tropical diseases, flicked over the pages and showed them the picture of the rat and of the flea.

'There is no doubt that Panya and Pani are real enemies. But there is a still smaller and more deadly enemy called Pestis, the *dudu*, the germ of the plague.'

I showed them the picture of the *dudu* in the book and then focused the microscope. There they were, that ominous chain of germs, both in the body of the crushed flea and in the gland of the dead rat.

The Chief shook his head. '*Yoh*, Bwana, this is a thing of amazement.'

'I tell you now, it is a disease that could kill thousands upon thousands of people in the plains of East Africa. But let no one be afraid. I have the medicine that deals with this disease. Anyone that has fever, anyone who has swollen glands, particularly here (my hand went to my groin)…let him come and we will give him medicine at once. Simba will explain to you the work that is yours for today. You have an enemy to kill and to destroy. This must be done carefully, relentlessly, ruthlessly.'

8

Fears and Fleas

Fear gripped the village. The people huddled outside the Chief's house in numb silence.

Simba stood to his feet and leaned on his spear. There was something about his smile and bearing which inspired confidence.

He addressed them in his deep voice. 'My friends and relations, let us lose our fear in doing things which bring safety. Also, let us have confidence in our weapons.'

He held up a large bottle of tablets.

'Here the Bwana has medicine which will deal with this great sickness. Let all of you who have swellings go to see him in the house made from canvas.' He pointed with his chin towards the tent.

'Those of you who have no sickness, here is a shield to protect you against it.' He held up an insect spray. 'Here in this pump-like machine is medicine to kill

Pani, the flea. It cannot harm you, for it is made from the kerosene we all buy for our lamps, mixed with the powdered petals of the Pyrethrum. There is no charm in it. There is no magic in it. It is *dudu*-poison which is harmless to people but deadly to fleas. See, Elisha will spray me first to prove to you it is harmless.'

The Chief stood forward. 'Spray me also.'

This started a general movement. Simba shouted, 'Stand up where you are, in a long line, and Elisha will come and spray you with this medicine of safety.'

He turned to Sumbili. 'Great One, I want a large fire built and over it put this oil drum. In this we will boil water and will keep it boiling. Into the drum must go each rat that is killed. Let nobody touch them with their hands but use a spear, or hold them with two sticks. These days flea bites can mean death. A dead rat is a good rat. A boiled flea is a safe flea. Dead rats and dead fleas mean that no way is left for dangerous *dudus* to attack.'

We went into action. A fire blazed under the oil drum and soon it was boiling. A nodding of heads and eager whispering showed that a new hope had come.

Perisi recorded everything, noting the time and counting the rats that were thrown in.

Four people with swollen glands came to the tent. Daudi wrote down their names, pulse rates and temperatures. With a syringe I took a little material from their swollen glands and examined

76

it under the microscope.

'Bwana,' said one of the men, 'are you sure that this is the right medicine?'

'*Eheh*, I am sure. I have complete confidence in it.'

'*Eheh*,' agreed Daudi, 'and so will you in a very short time. Sit there and put out your right hands.'

I placed eight pills into each hand. 'Chew them to powder, and drink.'

A variety of odd sounds accompanied the chewing and swallowing.

Slide after slide under the microscope confirmed what we feared. Many patients had plague. I focused on the last slide. Daudi's tense voice interrupted.

'Bwana, sit still. Don't move.' His hand flashed forward and his thumb pressed tightly over the bandage on my leg. Up slid his first finger and he grinned. 'Caught you, plague-carrier!' With his teeth he pulled the cork out of a medicine bottle and slipped his fingers over the neck. Down fell a small black something.

'Struggle, you brute!' said Daudi, putting back the cork.

I took the bottle and looked at the insect which hopped about futilely. 'You know, Daudi, that flea could have been coming or going as far as I am concerned.'

There was a little twist to the corner of my assistant's mouth. 'Doctor, you will report, will you not, if you find any swollen glands in your groins?'

The Chief sat quietly outside his house. I went across to him.

'Great One, how goes your trouble?'

He smiled. 'My breathing is becoming more difficult.'

I opened the small bottle of pills, put one into his hand and another onto my own tongue. We swallowed, sat down and chatted.

'*Yoh*, Bwana, there is thankfulness in my heart that this matter is being dealt with.'

'*Eheh*, the attack on the rats has already started. The next move is to burn medicine inside each house and drive out the brutes. We will block the doors and every place where air can get in. Panya and his relations will have no joy in the choking smoke.

'When the door opens they will bolt for the light and we will be ready. Poisoned rat food will be put in places where they will see it. It is a special poison to kill rats that does not hurt people or other animals. We will do all we can to wipe them out. We will also need a house for those who become sick tomorrow. It must be cleaned out completely so that no flea remains.'

Sumbili nodded. 'Bwana, this shall be done. Truly, the people are losing their fear.'

'I think, Bwana Mkubwa, they are losing their panic. They still have fear and they indeed have need for caution.'

Simba gathered a squad of some forty men and boys. They came to the first house and set about plugging up all gaps in the mud walls with old bits of cloth and tufts of grass.

He came across to me with a cut-down kerosene tin. 'Bwana, may I have a bag of the yellow medicine?'

'*Eheh*, you will find it in the large box marked No.3.

Open the bag and make sure it is the right stuff.'

From the box Simba took out and opened the bag, and inside was the yellow floury substance which was obviously sulphur.

'Bwana, I will put hot coals from the fire in here, place it in the middle of the house, pour sulphur onto it, and then run outside and block the door.'

'*Eheh*, let it burn for some time. Have the house surrounded in case any rat burrows its way out and then, as they come stumbling out, kill them and boil them. While you are waiting for the gas to take effect, order some of the men to move a little way from the village and dig a deep hole. Down that we will put the carcasses of the dead rats and also the dead hyaena that is now lying outside the house of the witchdoctor. Behold, many people now know that his way was one of deception.'

As Simba nodded he gave instructions and the digging started. To keep up the morale of the people Simba set a drummer to work. The rat hunters sang and carried the rhythm into their digging.

He came to report. 'All is ready, Bwana. The house is sealed up. In a minute now we will open the door.'

'*Viswanu* – good – but be very sure that no rat gets away.'

He smiled. 'See how we have arranged things, Bwana. First the house is surrounded by the nimble ones armed with sticks. Behind them is a second row of people standing close together. These are the women and the older men. If any rat escapes they will be almost certain to kill it. But to be completely sure the most agile and skilful in the village are outside them. If any enemy should pass the second line these *fundis* will finish it. See also, I have those who have spears or shovels. They will immediately carry the dead rat to the place of boiling.'

The drummer beat on enthusiastically.

Simba took the half kerosene tin to the fireplace and shovelled in some glowing coals. Then, taking a deep breath, he walked into the darkness of the house. Through the doorway I watched him tip the bag of sulphur onto the coals. There was a burst of blue flame.

Simba ran outside the door. He slammed it tight. Elisha carefully sprayed Simba with his insect killer from what the people called the *dudu*-pump.

'Sing!' shouted Simba. 'Sing and stamp upon the ground with enthusiastic feet. Bring confusion to the hearts of rats and misery to the legs of all fleas. Let everyone be in his place and ready – eyes open wide, sticks and spears poised.'

The whole village waited breathlessly for the opening door.

'Listen, everybody, the medicine that is in the house is not food for the nose. Breathe it, and it will make you cough and give you no joy. Keep well away from the place when the door is opened. Remember that in these days rats are more deadly than lions.'

Simba looked at me with raised eyebrows. 'Ready?'

Seeing my nod, he flung the door open. For five seconds nothing happened. Then four rats came out in a bunch. They were dead before they had travelled three metres. Two more erupted from the house. One almost escaped. Simba himself speared it as it scuttled past the second row of defence.

A small boy chanted, '*Saba, nane, kenda, kumi. kumi na moja* – seven, eight, nine, ten, eleven.' In all, fifteen rats came from that one house.

We had dealt with every house except the witchdoctor's. An hour before sunset, Perisi had put on her nurse's uniform and was looking after the women and girls who had the disease.

'Bwana,' she reported, 'we've slaughtered a hundred and sixty-two rats and there are nine sick people.'

Elisha limped up to me. 'Bwana, the first house that we cleaned up is ready to receive patients.'

'What is the floor made of, Elisha?'

'Mud and manure, pounded solid, Bwana.'

'Good. Fleas don't like that.'

'Words of truth, and no fleas live there now. We have sprayed it and sprayed it and sprayed it again.'

Daudi touched my shoulder. 'Doctor, look up there.'

High in the air over us hovered vultures. 'They know there is death in this village. Perhaps it is only the death of boiled rats.'

Daudi smiled. 'We will bury them all deep, and also that hyaena.'

A triumphant group marched to the pit and Simba dragged the dead hyaena by the tail. He suddenly swung it in the air. The boys laughed as it landed in the hole. They poured the hot water from the cauldron with its ugly contents of dead rats and shovelled more earth on top.

'*Yoh*,' shouted the people, 'they will never do any more harm.'

'Truly,' said Simba, 'we have killed and buried a death that could have taken many of us with it. Our work is to overcome death.' He stopped and pointed to the hills. The sun was setting behind them.

'Once Jesus came and died on a hill like that. They nailed him to a cross. He died to deal with the deadly disease of sin, which is much worse than plague. Some of your friends and relations are victims of this disease of plague and the Bwana is treating them. Others have escaped, but all have the disease of sin. No one but the Son of God can cure this sickness of the soul.'

There was an uneasy silence.

'This evening at the camp fire there will be singing. We will tell you words of great interest about rats and fleas and lions.'

'*Eheh*,' came a voice, 'and Bwana, will you tell us more about the Son of God?'

'We will indeed.'

9
Three Large and Three Small

Rat traps had been set all round the place, and dishes of bran mixed with poison were placed strategically.

Elisha reported to me. 'Bwana, I have finished two kerosene tins full of insect killer.'

'*Eheh*, that is a good thing. Line everyone up and spray them again tonight.'

'*Yoh*,' said Elisha, 'not only fleas, Bwana, but many other *dudus* will have no joy in our visit here.'

'*Eheh*, behold, there will be less scratching than there has been here for many a day.'

I went across to the Chief.

'Bwana,' he panted, 'tightness comes again to my chest.'

'Have one of the pills.'

He smiled and swallowed. '*Asante*—thank you, it is a medicine of strength.'

'I will leave more with you.' I pointed with my chin to the witchdoctor's house. 'There is one over there who must be filled with terror behind the mud walls of that house.' Sumbili nodded. 'Truly, death has been stalking in the darkness of that place.'

'Indeed, our greatest trouble may come from within those walls yet. That is why it is important to have guards there.'

Three of the leading men of the village were standing beside the Chief.

'Sumbili, let me explain.'

Elisha had opened a new tin of kerosene and was about to mix in the pyrethrum powder. 'Splash kerosene over the ground here, Elisha – lots of it.' He did so. 'The village is like this ground and dry grass. It is very ordinary. There seems to be no danger.'

They nodded in comprehension.

Suddenly I struck a match, and in a second flames were leaping over the ground. Simba came running to see what was happening. A puff of wind carried the flames on. They spread alarmingly. It took some minutes to bring everything under control again.

The Chief sat back panting. '*Yoh*, Bwana, that was a thing of danger.'

'Yes, true. It was my way of making you understand the danger we are all in. The house of the witchdoctor is like a box of matches. At any moment it could bring fire to the village which would spread like that flame.'

Even as we spoke, the wail of death came from the witchdoctor's house. People stood back. Terror again showed in their faces.

I walked with the Chief towards the ill-fated house and called at the top of my voice, 'O Pumba, can we help you?'

Silence.

I bent down and spoke to Daudi. He nodded his head. 'Doctor, they will bury their dead within the house. This is the habit of our people.'

The optimism of the people seemed to evaporate. In its place was near panic. Some villagers looked as if they would try running the gauntlet of the Chief's police. Then I saw Mboga. His fingers were flying over his *ilimba*. He was singing with vigour.

'To the camp fire!' called Daudi. 'Come round. The Bwana has words to pass on to you, words that will bring joy to your ears and comfort to your hearts.'

He put his hand on my arm. 'Bwana, when you talk to the people, talk gently. Help them understand. Tell them in pictures. Fear and fatigue are upon them. These things dull the mind and sharpen the temper.'

The Chief sat on a stool and placed another beside him for me.

The people looked at me sullenly. I took a long spear from one of the tribesmen, leant upon it and smiled at the people.

'Tell me, who in the jungle is the greatest? Is it Nhembo, the elephant, Simba, the lion or Chewi, the leopard?'

You could feel the people relax. A sound, part whisper, part laughter, rippled through my listeners.

Someone answered, 'Bwana, all these creatures are to be feared.'

'*Eheh*, I have heard of men climbing trees to escape Elephant, and arming themselves with spears and arrows to fight Lion and Leopard. But *yoh*, listen to my story.'

'Once Lion and Leopard and red-eyed Elephant met in the jungle. They told each other stories of their ferocity and the way they brought cold fear to the hearts of men. Elephant trumpeted, "I come with my ears flapping, my trunk waving and my great tusks prepared to crush and tear. *Yoh*, how they run when they hear the voice of red-eyed Elephant."

'Leopard snarled to show off his frightening teeth. "My voice is all I need to use," he sneered. "When they hear the deep sound of my snarl, men run in panic. *Hueegh*, they scream, for their blood turns to water."

'Lion turned up his nose. "If your voice does what you say, what do you think happens when I roar?"

'From a small hole between two large rocks, Panya the rat greeted them. "Truly, you are the mighty lords of the jungle, of majesty and of muscle. But I, and my two helpers, we all fit comfortably in this small hole. We call ourselves the three Ps. I, Panya the rat, speak for the other two whose voices are not loud enough for your ears. Their names are Pani the flea, and Pestis the *dudu*. We three small ones challenge you, creatures of muscle and might, to a test of strength for three days. Let us attack man in his house."

'Elephant lifted up his trunk and laughed a deep laugh. "We will trumpet and snarl and roar. We will trample and tear with trunk and tusk and tooth. What can you do, O Rat? The smallest pressure of my foot, and you are squashed flatter than a leaf."

"It is even as you say," said Rat without anger. "But let us see who does more damage to the lives of men. You three, Elephant, Lion and Leopard, or we small three, Panya, Pani and the little *dudu*, Pestis."

'And so it was agreed. For the first three days the large animals used their large voices until the jungle shook. They were days of terror. Men armed themselves with spears and arrows and flaming torches.

'*Nhembo*, the elephant, worked himself into a rage. His little eyes were red, his trunk swayed to and fro and his huge ears flapped. He pounded down the path tearing the limbs off trees. He crashed through the cornfields, squashing them flat, tearing up cornstalks in his anger. He came to a house. With his great shoulders he pushed the wall in. With his front feet he crushed the grain storage bin. With his trunk he grasped a man and beat him to death on the ground. The whole village rose to attack. Men took their spears and their arrows, and with skill and courage and subtlety they drove Elephant back into the jungle.

'Leopard sprang from a leaf-covered branch and killed a goatherd. The sound of his snarl by night kept every door in the jungle shut. Spears were sharpened and were close to the hands of scores of strong men by day and night. Lion came at dusk, and though he killed with each huge paw as he sprang among those who sat round the camp fire, he was driven from the village with flaming torches.

'The third day, Panya came to them. "Rest your voices, mighty ones. Relax your overworked bodies while we three do our work."

'The large animals were too tired to laugh. They sat

in the green shade while Panya scuttled through the short grass into the village. Men were rebuilding the houses Elephant had destroyed. Others lay in the sun with drawn faces, enduring the pain of the wounds produced by Lion's teeth and Leopard's claws. No one even bothered to notice Panya.

'He stopped under the shelter of a corn bin and said to Pani, who hopped onto a suitable portion of his tail, "The voice of sorrow is soon stilled after the work of those with big legs. Now let us work."

'Flea nodded. "The plan is simple. There is no need for you, O Rat, to use your teeth. Your work is to carry me to places while I play my part and carry Pestis, who is a very small creature indeed, so small that neither your eyes nor mine can see him. Men have little fear of you, Panya. They merely order the small boys to throw things at you. They are irritated by me, not frightened. In their talk round the camp fire they laugh at those of small courage and say, 'He is so harmless he couldn't hurt a flea."

"What is true of us is even truer of our third helper, the *dudu* Pesitis. No one fears him or even thinks about him. If he is too small for us to see, what chance have the dull eyes of man?"

"Let us to work then," came the tiny voice of the plague *dudu*. "Panya, creep to the places where men sit and sleep. Pani, leap upon them and bite them so that they may scratch their skin with their clumsy hands. Then poison the places where they scratch and foul them with the filth of your body. In this way, O my partners, we will find opportunity to kill in a way undreamed of by Lion and Leopard and Elephant – and man."

'There was something completely deadly in the tiny voice of the plague germ which went on, "Your tribe, Panya, breeds with speed. In weeks your sons are fathers. You, Pani, may lay thousands of eggs that hatch out in days, but in our family this happens in twenty minutes; every twenty minutes, each one of us becomes two. So between sunrise and sunrise one of us becomes countless millions. Come, Panya, come, Pani. To the task!"

'Through the village scurried, jumped and crept small deadly creatures. Fever came to the people of the village. Swellings appeared. Their sickness became severe. Their bodies shivered and their strength disappeared. Behold, the sounds of death were heard right through the countryside.

'At the end of three days Rat sat back. Flea hopped out on Panya's tail and said, "There. In three days a thousand have been put on the road to death by the efforts of us, the three small ones. The large ones crush and tear, snarl and trumpet, and half-a-dozen people die. We make no sound. We bite with teeth that cause no pain, and a thousand die."

'From their small throats came terrible laughter which was so soft that nobody heard and nobody feared.'

I paused. The faces were intent upon what I was saying.

'Today, in your village of Matama, Panya the rat is more dangerous than any angry elephant.'

10
Rat Catchers

A small, pitifully thin dog looked at me through the doorway and grinned – a definitely cheerful grin. There was a question in his large brown eyes.

I snapped my fingers and said in Chigogo, '*Mbukwa, Chibwa* – Good day, small dog.'

The curled tail started to wag, as did most of his skinny frame.

I laughed. '*Yoh!* Truly, you are a head and tail kept apart by little more than a famine.'

The grin seemed to enlarge and the tail to move even more enthusiastically.

'You could do with a large and meaty bone, Chibwa, and you could be more than a help in this rat hunt if you choose to help.'

Then I realised that I was not talking to a dog only, for a twelve-year-old boy had moved out of the shadows. He spoke with fear in his voice. 'Bwana, do dogs catch this sickness of death?'

'Fortunately, no.'

'*Yoh*, that is food for our ears. We had fears, he and I.'

'*Hongo*, do you feed him regularly?'

The boy stepped clear of the doorway and I saw that he himself was as undernourished as the dog.

'When there is food, Bwana, we share it.'

I nodded. '*Eheh*. Now, suppose I offer you both a rat-hunting job. I will pay three meals a day for both man and dog.'

His eyes sparkled. '*Swanu muno muno*. It is a thing of joy, Bwana. We…'

'O dog with tail of considerable energy,' I broke in, 'would you use your ivory teeth to bring suitable damage to the family of Panya, the rat?'

It seemed to me that the small animal understood every word I spoke, for he tilted his head to one side and looked at the boy who said, 'Bwana, you like dogs?'

'*Eheh*, very much.'

'Chibwa likes you, too, Bwana. How did you know his name?'

'I guessed because he was a small dog. Now tell me, what is yours?'

'They call me *Chimate*.' Silently I translated. 'Little Spit.'

'What is your father's name?'

'He is dead, Bwana.'

'Your mother?'

'She is also with the ancestors.'

'Where do you live?'

'Here and there, Bwana. People have small joy in me. Am I not a child of ill luck? Do not the spirits mark me? Am I not a person of shame?'

The dog moved close to him and licked his hand. He caressed its long ears.

Defiantly he pulled the back cloth from his shoulder and half turned. There was a fist-shaped swelling at the end of his spine.

'Don't you see, Bwana?'

'Yes, Chimate, I see. But tell me, will you and Chibwa here work for me in this battle against sickness?'

The cloth was slowly draped again, but he beamed. '*Koh*, Bwana, we will. We will work with joy.'

'That's excellent, but first you must be given a new name. This is work for those of skill. I will call you *Kisu* - the hunting knife.'

A smile spread over his face. He ran his fingers gently up the dog's back and said, '*Koh*, Chibwa. This is a thing of wonder…a new name for me and work of value to do.'

'And food to start with after one special thing happens.'

Four eyes turned to me suddenly, expectantly.

'Rats have fleas. Fleas hate water and soap. Fleas are hard to hit, harder still to see. They are our enemies. All my helpers wash often and carefully. Here is hot water and soap. Now go to it.'

As Chibwa was lathered, an experience that was obviously unique to him, he took on a look of complete resignation to a horrible fate. He closed his eyes piously as water was poured over him. His whole bearing made me shake with laughter.

Kisu looked at me doubtfully. His eyes followed mine to the small dog and he saw the funny side of the situation. When he laughed he seemed a different person.

'You're next, Kisu, and then food.'

We went to a sheltered corner by a large baobab tree, and with his dog standing watching at what he considered a safe distance, he too bathed.

I produced two lengths of white cloth and threw them to the boy. 'Throw your old ones into the fire lest they contain fleas. Wear these, and here is food.'

Boy and dog sat and ate solemnly while I worked with the microscope.

A deep sigh came at last, and Kisu smiled and said, '*Twa*!' which is a useful word to indicate that a bottle is full to the neck.

He walked over to me. 'Bwana, what about my lump?'

'It's something I'm most interested in.'

94

'Bwana, you didn't talk about it or draw away or look strange.'

'I did not. Lumps like this can be removed without pain. But for the moment it's rats. We will deal with lumps later. Dust this powder over Chibwa and hunt with vigour, but don't touch rats with your hands. Here is a tin with a lid for your catch.'

I watched boy and dog walk purposefully away.

Mboga came to the door. 'Two new sick ones, Bwana.'

An hour later as I scrubbed my hands, Simba walked across to me.

'*Yoh*, Bwana, trouble. The people are beginning to grumble. There is too much time on their hands and too many fears in their heads.'

'Tell me the answer, Lion-killer.'

'Food for the stomach and food for the ears, Bwana.'

'Good medicine, truly, but where is it to be found?'

'Roasted meat, Bwana.'

'*Mmmm*! A full stomach is a strong antidote to fear!'

'The *askari* sergeant would shoot a couple of buck and…'

I nodded. 'Wisdom of high order. I shall write a note.'

It read:

Fundi Sergeant,

Your rifle speaks a word that could bring joy to the

stomachs of many. Will you cause it to talk twice? A little meat would lighten the burden of the guard and quieten the restlessness in the village. May your trigger finger be skilful.

Simba chuckled as I read it over to him. 'That will produce results, Bwana.'

'So much for stomachs. What about ears?'

'*Gramophoni*, Bwana, and the black plates that go round and round. The new ones that tell about God and sing songs will keep people listening hour after hour.'

'*Hongo*, Simba. Your wisdom has strength today.'

'*N'go*, Bwana. These are Perisi's ideas. *Heee*! She sees far ahead.'

'Bwana,' called a voice behind me, 'another tin, please. This is filled *twa*! With the enemy.'

Kisu moved the lid a little and showed it packed full with dead rats.

'Chibwa is more nimble than a leopard in chasing rats.'

'*Hongo*,' agreed Simba, 'he is an animal of merit.'

Kisu beamed. 'A little thin perhaps, but truly nimble.'

'Size and strength will come with food.' I smiled. 'And Daudi, my special helper, and Simba, the lion hunter, will have joy to welcome you to our team.'

Simba nodded solemnly. 'Kisu is truly a good name for a hunter.'

'The Bwana gave it to me. Many still call me Chimate, but...'

'The Bwana was right. Here, take my light spear and carry this message to the *askari* sergeant for me. Tonight we would taste meat roasted.'

Both boy and dog grinned. '*Yoh*, a thing of much joy. But what of the rat hunting?'

'Carry the message with feet that raise dust. Return without prolonged greeting.'

Kisu hurried off clutching his spear and holding the note wedged in a split stick.

Daudi was smiling. 'A boy of worth, Bwana.'

'Truly. He has joy today for the first time for a long while.'

'Bwana,' called Perisi, 'two more sick ones.'

But both were only moderately sick. People were coming earlier now, and the earlier we started treatment the better.

As I counted pills into Perisi's hand, we heard the report of a rifle, followed not long after by another.

The village was excited. The cold hand of fear was losing its grip. A pile of firewood was evidence of preparations for a barbecue. The singing went on cheerfully.

Up the hill, struggling under a load of meat, came Kisu, Chibwa in close attendance. The singing suddenly stopped and people came running over to help carry the rest of the feast.

Mboga still stood on guard outside the witchdoctor's house. His fingers were busy on his *ilimba*.

I walked over to him. His playing became louder and in hoarse whisper he spoke.

'Bwana, there are strange happenings in the witchdoctor's house. It is a place of darkness and danger.'

11
Flea Bite

The feast was a resounding success. It was astonishing how much food could disappear in so short a time. Simba pulled a piece of meat from the bone he was dealing with and tossed it in the direction of the small dog, who swallowed it in one gulp and grinned.

'*Yoh*,' laughed the hunter, 'a creature of content, that.'

Kisu, his mouth full, nodded, his eyes glowing.

Drums, whistles and *ilimbas* had appeared, and the musicians started up as the feasting slowed a little.

Kisu picked up his spear and a knobbed stick, whistled to the dog, whispered in Simba's ear, and walked away.

'He has set many traps, Bwana, and goes to check them. He is a boy of understanding.'

He moved over to the fire and put on a kerosene tin half filled with water.

A figure came out from the dancers, struck a pose and then started to sing a song composed for my special benefit.

I bowed my thanks and said, 'I have joy in your rejoicing. To sing is good. To resist trouble is good. Yours is a village of courage. Let us fight on with our bodies strengthened by food and our ears comforted by those who sing and produce music with nimble fingers.'

'*Hongo*,' said Daudi, 'the Bwana has brought a machine of wonder to bring the deepest joy and comfort to all of you. It is in a box which you feed by turning a handle. Upon the box circles a shining black plate. Touch this with an arm of metal and music comes, voices also. When we have heard your singing a little longer, we will bring this machine of amazement for your eyes to see and your ears to hear.'

Carefully he produced the gramophone and showed them its various features.

There was a chorus of *Yoh*! *Kumbe*! and *Hongo*! as interested faces tried to catch a glimpse of the machine. Then the pick-up touched the disc and their mouths opened soundlessly.

Before the record finished, a hand touched mine.

'Bwana, the nose of Chibwa has found a strange thing in the house of Pumba.'

'Well done, Kisu! This is a thing of importance.'

He smiled and Daudi whispered, 'He has joy today, doctor. Not often does he hear words of praise.'

Into the bubbling oil drum over the blazing fire, Kisu tipped sixteen rats. 'Twelve caught in the traps,

Bwana. The others we chased out of holes. No rat can escape Chibwa.'

The record ended. Daudi was about to turn it over when the door of the witchdoctor's house was pushed open and out stalked Pumba. His cheek bones were gaunt and he looked like a walking skeleton. On his head was a buffalo-skin headdress. A string of leopard's teeth was round his neck. He laughed a high-pitched hysterical laugh. Following him came the old woman who worked with him. If ever I saw a model for a witch, she was it. Astride a drum, she started to chant in a way that was hair-raising.

Without saying a word, Pumba took off his cowhide sandals, spat on them, slowly turned and looked, it seemed, at every individual in the village. People cowered. He had the odd ability to make fear erupt like a volcano. His feet kept time with the uncanny rhythm of the old woman's drum. Then his voice, cracked and dry, repeated the one word again and again…

'*Nani… nani… nani…*? Who… who… who…?'

Flecks of froth appeared at the corners of his mouth. There was a wildness in his eye that looked suspiciously like high fever.

Daudi whispered, 'He's caught it, doctor. *Yoh,* this means deep trouble.'

Mboga stood rigidly outside the witchdoctor's mud-and-wattle house, his stick raised. Then a nod passed between him and Simba and Daudi.

'Doctor,' my assistant whispered, 'keep things going here with much talk and, whatever happens, keep their interest away from that house.'

Mboga slipped through the door into the dangerous darkness of Pumba's house and the door closed quietly after him.

Ten seconds later, with a yell, the frenzied witchdoctor spat on his sandals and threw them into the air. They landed, both pointing to the spot where Mboga had been. Eyes followed the direction that the sandals and the chin of the witchdoctor indicated but nobody was there.

'He shall die – die!' screamed the harsh voice and the drum suddenly stopped.

I jumped to my feet. 'This is a matter of no profit.' I wrenched off a shoe, threw it into the air and caught it. 'It is a thing of small skill to make my shoe fall so that it points towards anybody I choose. It is all a matter of practice.'

'Watch this, O people of Matama. Watch this, and if Pumba has wisdom equal to it, then and only then take notice.'

In the medicine bag was a small, powerful magnet. Without being seen I pushed this into the folds of bandage that covered my thigh. Then, taking a large sheet of firm paper, I spread it over my knees and motioned to Elisha to give me a long nail that he kept in his tightly curled hair.

The people moved around me warily.

'There, O Chief, is a long iron nail lying all by itself. But should I wish, the point of it will turn to me when it hears the magic words.' In English I chanted,

'Humpty-Dumpty sat on a wall,

Humpty-Dumpty had a great fall.

All the King's horses and all the King's men,

Couldn't put Humpty together again.'

Up came my thigh under the paper, the magnet came into action and the nail swung towards me.

There was an amazed whispering that grew into a thin sound full of fear.

'Tell me, O Nail, who is the Great One of this village?'

The nail, following the unnoticed movement of my leg, pointed straight to Sumbili.

'*Yoh*,' came a score of scared voices, 'this is witchcraft!'

'*Heeeeh*!' screamed Pumba, 'he moves it with his finger!'

Daudi shrugged his shoulders. 'The Bwana will put his hand above his head.'

I did so.

'Order the nail, O Pumba,' said Simba.

'*Kah*,' said the witchdoctor, and spat, 'who is the cause of all this trouble?'

The nail did not move.

'Bwana,' said the Chief after a while, 'ask the nail where the danger lies.'

The nail slowly swung round to the witchdoctor's long hut. Overhead flew an owl. It hovered soundlessly above the doorway.

A sudden yell came from the people and Pumba stood with staring eyes. A rat scuttled out into the night. Elisha swung round and rammed a bucket over it.

The village sprang into action and the house was surrounded. I walked across to the wild-eyed African and put my hand on his shoulder. He was burning hot. His legs gave way and it was all I could do to save him from falling heavily. His chest was moving oddly and he coughed a strange-sounding cough.

'Morphia, Daudi, a quarter grain. Pumba has the disease in his lung. He's more dangerous now than a cartload of rats. He can breathe out, cough out, sneeze out, millions of germs.'

I drew from my pocket a length of gauze and held it in my palm in case he should sneeze or cough.

Daudi came running with the syringe. As I injected, the old woman who sat watching everything like a statue, screamed, 'The European's killing him, killing him, killing him!'

The Chief shook her. 'Quiet!' With a look that was almost a sneer she squatted down and beat the drum in a dirge-like rhythm.

The Chief queried, 'What's happening, Bwana?'

'This is trouble, severe sickness. The disease is in his lung. He could kill everyone in the place with the germs he coughs out.'

'Let him die then, Bwana.'

'No!'

'But perhaps he will give you trouble!'

'We will try to save him.'

'Does anyone ever recover?'

'Very few, but these days we have a special medicine.'

From the witchdoctor's house came shouting.

'Bwana.' Simba came running over. 'The place is alive with fleas. They were all over Mboga, hundreds of them. Elisha has sprayed round the place with vigour, but it is a place of death.'

'Let us burn it to the ground,' said Sumbili. 'It is a place of danger.'

He looked down at the unconscious figure. For a moment his eyes gleamed with satisfaction and I sensed that these two were bitter enemies.

12

Leopard Changes Spots

'Pile thornbushes round the place, grass, anything that will burn. We'll spray kerosene over the whole place.'

'Are you sure no one is inside, Mboga?'

'Nobody, Bwana. I looked everywhere except in the grain bin.' He grinned. 'Nobody would ever think of hiding in those great wickerwork bins. The boy and the dog must have been mistaken about someone who snored. Behold, their ears were deceived by the sound of the drums.'

Kisu gripped my arm. 'Bwana, there was something there. In these things the nose of dogs is beyond the wisdom of men.'

Daudi touched my shoulder. 'Doctor,' he whispered, 'it was in these bins that Pumba kept honey spirit. He made this of such strength that two of those who drank it slept the sleep of death and others followed the way of baboons.'

'Let's make certain, anyway. Simba, tear a hole in the roof and look down before we set fire to the place.'

He vaulted onto the roof and started with a will.

The old woman who beat the drum for the witchdoctor shrieked shrilly. With amazing speed she rushed to the door and beat on it with her fists. Daudi moved across quickly and firmly steered her away from that house of danger. She kicked and scratched and would have bitten him had he not been nimble.

People crowded around as she went sullenly back to her drum-beating.

Perisi came up behind me. 'Bwana, she makes all this fuss because in that house are many of her medicines: the intestines of crocodiles, burnt and made into strong and deadly charms, the same thing made from the heart of poisoned snakes and from the powdered teeth of leopards. There is much of black magic and wickedness and poison in that house. Truly, it is the companion of plague and deadliness and death. We will cleanse the village in two ways if that place is burnt to ashes. It...'

Her mouth opened wide in amazement as she saw Simba, standing on the roof of the house, leap back in alarm as through the hole that he had hacked came a grotesque figure. The man's eyes rolled horribly. He let out a bull-like roar and then collapsed.

'*Yoh*,' said Elisha, 'it is Palata, drunk on honey spirit and crazy as a mad monkey.'

'Simba,' I cried, 'keep him up there till Elisha has sprayed him. He must be alive with fleas.'

'*Heh*,' came back Simba's voice in disgust, 'no flea would be so unwise as to touch Palata and, Bwana, if they had bitten him they would be drunk now. *Heeeh*, he's full of alcohol. If I were to strike a match near him now he would go up in flames. *Yoh*!'

In the excitement the old woman pushed Daudi out of the way, threw herself against the door of the hut and snatched up a banana-leaf-wrapped parcel. She held it close to her withered chest, then dashed down the hill from the village.

'Daudi,' I urged, 'alert the guards. Make absolutely sure that she does not get through that cordon of *askaris*.'

He ran. I climbed on the roof and shone a torch down. Now that Palata had come out from the place it was obvious that there was nobody left in that sinister witchdoctor's house. With a stirrup-pump I sprayed kerosene inside, put a match to an oil-soaked rag and threw it down into the plague-infested darkness. In a few seconds the whole place was a roaring inferno. The rat-hunters moved swiftly and no rodent escaped.

Chibwa and Kisu stood at the ready. Daudi had placed three stripes of sticking plaster on the boy's bare arm giving him the rank of sergeant-hunter, to his considerable pleasure.

A snake slid, hissing angrily, out from the burning hut, moving like a flash. The people leapt aside in panic. Simba dashed through them waving his stick,

but Chibwa got there first. He leapt and buried his teeth in the reptile's neck. A rat hurtled out of the house and would have been lost but for the little dog. He looked up at Simba as if to say, 'Over to you,' and letting go of the snake he shot off after the rat. A minute later he returned with it, dead, between his teeth. His tail moved in a way that left no doubt about his feelings.

As the little dog was being solemnly sprayed, Sumbili came over to me.

'Bwana, truly we are watching events that will bring peace and health to this village.'

'Those are words of truth, but remember it is not enough merely to sweep out evil. The ways of God must come into your hearts and the Son of God, Jesus Christ himself, must be Chief, not only of your village but of each of the people in it.'

He nodded. At that moment from down the hill came the all-too-familiar danger signal.

'Bwana, come quickly. There is trouble.' It was Daudi's voice, loud in the distance.

Halfway between the village and the circle of African police was a pile of boulders surrounded by tall, dry

112

tufty grass and more thornbush. The old woman had made for this and disappeared.

Simba and Mboga, each clutching a spear, ran ahead to help Daudi. Sumbili and I walked more slowly behind and had almost come to this unusual pile of rock when from the middle of it sprang a leopard. It passed within a hand's breadth of Mboga, who fell over backwards in his excitement. Taking no notice, it bounded past the guarding circle. In a second it flashed past and disappeared into the undergrowth.

'*Yoh*,' muttered Simbili, '*heh*, I have seen it with my own eyes. She became a leopard and is gone.'

N'go, Great One. She is hiding in there. She has hidden carefully and disturbed the leopard in its lair.'

The Chief shook his head and clutched at my arm as an owl, blinking in the sunlight, flew out of the rocks.

'*Yoh*, Bwana, there is her messenger, Tuwi, the owl. There is much witchcraft with owls.'

He turned and hurried away from me up the hill.

'Quickly, Simba, run back. Make sure the men of the village do not stop guarding that blazing hut. If fleas spread around the village all our good work is wasted.'

Mboga was slowly getting to his feet. '*Yoh*,' he said, carefully removing cactus spikes from his patched trousers, 'this is a plant of rarity in this country of ours, but behold, where should I choose to fall but upon it!'

'Oh, forget the cactus. There are things of great importance happening.'

'*Eheh*, it's easy for you, Bwana, but you do not have a score of burning needles sticking into you.'

I grinned. '*Yoh*, Spinach cannot be overgrown by cactus, surely!'

There was a hidden chuckle in Mboga's voice as he said, 'Truly, Bwana, you bear my sufferings with great courage.'

I turned to Daudi. 'What about this leopard problem?'

He shook his head. 'Bwana, everyone in the village will believe that she has become a leopard.'

'That may well be, but my feeling is that she is hiding behind a stone or crouching down behind some of that dense undergrowth.'

Daudi and I walked back to the village. Simba hurried towards us. 'Bwana, the leopard has frightened the people. They will panic unless we do something to take their minds off it.'

'*Eheh*, Simba. Why don't you and Mboga stir them into activity. Keep them hunting for rats. Keep them digging the brutes out of the ground with their hoes and axes. Keep them singing one of those cultivation songs with a lot of rhythm in it. Let's hide their fear in song and action.'

Mboga left off hunting for cactus spikes and dashed ahead of Daudi. In a few minutes he was swinging a hoe, leading the village in another rat hunt.

The kindness and competence of my helpers was so impressive that in half an hour the village was calm again. I walked across to the smouldering ruins of the witchdoctor's hut. Only the charred hardwood main posts remained upright. The mud-plastered wicker-work had become dust, ashes and lumps of hard-baked earth. The glowing embers were all that remained of a place branded with black magic and black death.

Kisu came and stood beside me. He looked up at the blueness of the tropical sky and with his chin he pointed high in the air to a spot directly over the pile of boulders where the old woman had disappeared.

'See them, Bwana?'

Vultures were circling high in the air.

'Bwana, something other than witchcraft interests those birds of death...'

13

Bones and Empty Bottles

Towards us, running helter-skelter with his small dog keeping carefully behind, came Kisu.

'Bwana,' he panted, 'it is a thing of deep fear.' He shivered and Chibwa crouched at his feet.

'What did you see that causes this alarm?'

'It is the bones that lie all in place, not old dry ones but new ones, new bones that...' He couldn't find the word he wanted, and finished, 'Chibwa found them.'

'We'd better go and see what it is, Bwana,' said Simba.

'It is a thing of death or vultures would not circle,' said Daudi as we walked down the hill.

Kisu pointed with his chin to a concealed gap between the granite boulders. In a place where the rock sloped sharply was the grotesque sight of a skeleton, the flesh neatly stripped from the bones. So expertly was this done that I was at a loss to understand it.

Simba spoke. 'I have seen that happen before. It is the work of Masiafu, the ants. A lion's kill can become a skeleton in a night. They are small, these ants, but they come by the hundreds of thousands. They work quietly but with terrible thoroughness. The old woman must have been attacked by the leopard. Is not her arm broken? She fell unconscious and…' He shrugged. There was no need to put words to the grim picture. We walked slowly back to the village.

Perisi came hurrying towards me. 'Bwana, there is trouble here. Four new sick ones have come. That is sixteen in all, and Pumba, the witchdoctor – *ehhh*! His sickness is great upon him.'

'I will come at once, Perisi.'

'Simba, ask Sumbili to go with you down into the rocks there. He must see that this is not a matter of witchcraft but of the rugged ways of the jungle.'

In the hut that we were using as an emergency hospital Elisha had made holes in the walls and put in fly-wire-covered window frames. In the dim light I could see Pumba lying on a native bed propped up on pillows that were nothing but cheap cotton material stuffed with grass. I put a mask made in the shape of a bag over my head. There were eyeholes in it. Over these I pulled goggles. On lifting the double mosquito net it became obvious that Pumba was breathing like someone with pneumonia. The stethoscope told me the story of heavy infection, and I knew that his lungs were swarming with myriads of plague germs.

I heard Perisi's voice over my shoulder. 'Bwana, they say that many times he has had sickness in his chest.'

'He has the most deadly disease that I know of – plague in his lung. We call it pneumonic plague.'

'How do you treat it, Bwana? With many pills?'

'To try and overcome it with mere pills would be like trying to put out a grass fire with a gourdful of water. Thank God, we also have strong injectable drugs.'

Perisi spoke quickly. 'Bwana, Simba, my husband, and also Mboga have had pneumonia. Would it not be wise to give them medicine in case the disease has affected them even a little?'

'*Eheh*, Perisi, that is a word of wisdom. Find them both and give them each four of the pills to take at once and another four at sunset.'

Looking relieved she hurried away.

I loaded the syringe from one of the four little glass ampoules labelled 'streptomycin'. Pumba made no move as I injected, but the whites of his eyes rolled and he muttered words that I had never heard before. He seemed to be trying to escape from something.

I stood watching him for a couple of minutes. He seemed to fall into an uneasy sleep, but his chest moved up and down at three times the normal speed.

Mboga came to the door, took one look at me and started to run. Then he stopped. '*Yoh*, Bwana, you scared me! *Heh*, you look awful with that white cloth over your face and those strange things over your eyes. You would bring fear even to the strongest.'

I took off the mask and goggles, carefully scrubbing my hands.

'Mboga, I have work for you to do. First, have you swallowed the pills?'

'*Eheh*, Bwana. It was for this reason that I came to see you. Was I to take four pills or eight?'

'Four now and four at sunset.'

'*Yoh*, but, Bwana, I have taken eight.'

I laughed. '*Heh*, all the better. I wanted to make sure that none of these germs found their way into your system.'

Mboga looked at the sick figure of the witchdoctor. '*Heh*, I too have this same wish. There is little profit in looking as he looks or suffering as he suffers.'

'You speak the truth. Now, make yourself useful. Music and singing will keep the village busy working. Get them to work and keep them at it.'

He went outside, and a few moments later I could hear the singing of some of the cultivation songs, Mboga in the lead.

I went around to the sick ones, listening to chests, examining swollen glands, checking hearts, looking for enlarged livers and spleens and pressing on shin bones to see if there was any swelling.

Perisi made a note of my instructions.

I looked at her carefully. 'Perisi, you had better rest. There was no sleep for you last night and all day long you have been working.'

She smiled. 'Bwana, I still have strength.'

'Have sleep, however, for who knows what may happen in the night before us?'

Outside, the brick-makers were hard at work. Mboga was cheering them on. Up the hill came the Chief and Simba walking slowly and talking earnestly together. Elisha was keeping a watch over the patients.

'*Yoh*,' said Sumbili coming up to me, 'Bwana, behold now we understand. The old woman must have disturbed the leopard as she hid among the boulders. He struck her with his paw and she fell unconscious.'

'Perhaps,' said Simba, 'it was the ants who disturbed Leopard for, behold, even Chewi himself will not wait when Masiafu march like an army with their small teeth that bite to grim effect. Anyway, it was not a thing of black magic.'

The Chief put his hand on his chest. 'Bwana, *eeeh*, I have difficulty in breathing after climbing that steep hill.'

I gave him four more pills. 'Use these as you need them, Sumbili. Behold, in front of me is much trouble and even more work. There are eighteen people now with this sickness and Pumba, behold, his sickness is full of danger.'

The Chief frowned. 'Bwana. He followed the ways of the devil and yet you work hard for his life.'

'*Ngheeh*! Why do it?' echoed Simba.

'It is the way of God. Jesus Christ, the Son of God, said himself, "Love your enemies, do good to those that hate you." They were not empty words, for he himself died that his enemies could be forgiven and go free. His instructions to those that would travel his way are "follow me".'

'*Yoh*,' said the Chief, 'few words, truly.'

'They are words easy to understand but hard to carry out.'

'Behold, they have high value in them,' said Simba.

The sun was setting. Mboga, surrounded by people, was playing his *ilimba*.

Elisha came across to me. 'Bwana, witchdoctor is worse.'

I hurried to the ward and went to the double-mosquito-net-covered bed where the delirious witchdoctor lay. Spasms shook his chest when he coughed. Hastily I covered his mouth with a wad of gauze. This I threw into a tin and forced down the lid. There were enough deadly germs on that gauze to wipe out the whole village. Pumba sank back on the pillow. His pulse was well over two hundred. He was breathing forty times to the minute.

I gave him another ampoule of streptomycin and a second injection to quiet the coughing and bring sleep and rest. It took ten long minutes for the medication to take effect, and keeping that frenzied witchdoctor in bed was no easy matter. He was throwing himself about in delirium. I caught the words 'hyaena' and 'owl'. Again and again came the phrase, '*Mahala matitu*… Black magic… Black magic,' and then some mumbling about a box.

Daudi's voice behind me said, 'Bwana, he must know that his house has been burnt down. He has hot anger, for he has lost many of his strongest medicines like love potions ground from rhino horn.'

'*Yoh*, this is an evil thing, Daudi.'

Outside the singing was still going on. Mboga was keeping the village thoroughly occupied.

Perisi brought her ward report. 'Bwana, nothing new has happened. There are still some high temperatures.'

We went over the charts together and I gave out various medicines and pills.

The singing stopped at last, and I listened to the friendly sound of crickets with an occasional bullfrog adding his trombone-like noises in the background.

At midnight the crickets and frogs were still active, but the village was silent except for the coughing and turning of sick people and the deep breathing of Daudi who had fallen asleep on the chair where he sat.

I shook down a thermometer, put it under the witchdoctor's arm and held it in place for two complete minutes. The silver line of the mercury had climbed in the thermometer to almost 41°C.

Two of the ampoules of streptomycin were empty. I filled the syringe with the third and injected it. It was swelteringly hot in the protective garments.

A touch on Daudi's shoulder was enough to wake him. 'Daudi, I am going to snatch three hours sleep. Will you keep a watch on things, particularly on old Pumba? His temperature is high. Take it again at three o'clock and let me know what it is when you wake me at that hour.'

He nodded. 'Doctor, I will keep walking around. Behold, fatigue has me in its grip.'

'Me also, Daudi. We will each sleep a few hours at a time and pray God for strength to see this thing through.'

Without undressing I flopped down on a mattress in the back of the truck, wrapped myself in a blanket and made sure there were no mosquitoes in the net. In a minute I was asleep.

I slumbered so heavily that Daudi had to shake hard to wake me up.

'Doctor, it is the ninth hour of the night,' which is another way of saying 3 a.m. 'You said to wake you.'

I stumbled heavily to my feet and yawned. '*Eheh*, Daudi. How is everybody?'

'Pumba is worse. His pulse you cannot count. His breathing is forty-four. His temperature is 41°C.'

'*Yoh*, Daudi, there is only one thing for it. He must have the last injection. If that doesn't bring his temperature down there is nothing we can do.'

I came into the ward and sprayed the double mosquito-net that covered the witchdoctor's bed. It was vital that no germs should be lurking in the air for anyone to breathe. In this way death could come easily and infection would be spread like a flood through the country.

As the last injection was given, I prayed that there might be enough of the drug to deal with the witchdoctor's infection. His life was such that if his body died, his soul must inevitably perish also. I thought of the clear-cut words St John had written, 'He that has the Son has life and he that has not the Son of God has not life.'

Pumba had lined up his life and living with the devil. Some more words sprang to my mind, 'Sin always pays its servants. Those wages are death.'

Pumba had collected nearly the whole of what he was owed.

'*Malenga* – water!' called a voice from the other side of the hut. I carefully took off my protective hood and goggles, placed the empty streptomycin ampoule with its three fellows, and went across the ward to give a small boy a drink from a gourd.

'Pills,' I said, putting two into his hand. 'Chew them up and swallow them.'

He nodded and his eyes lit up as he saw me move across and pick up a lump of brown sugar the size of a ping-pong ball. I went round the ward handing out pills, waking people up. It is not a good thing to wake folk up who are sick, but unless those pills were taken regularly, the plague germs would flourish and kill.

For a while there was a certain amount of talk, then sleep came again and silence with it.

I went out into the cool of the night. The moon had disappeared over the horizon. The far off roar of a lion broke through the stillness. I stood there and prayed, 'O God, help us to save these lives.'

Then I prayed for my wife and children and looked out towards the east, towards the jungle hospital where I knew all manner of difficulties might well be cropping up. There was need for a dozen doctors, not one. There was scope for a score of jungle nurses.

How tremendously thankful I was to those who had sent the money for the medicines which made it possible for us to break the back of the plague epidemic! I thanked God for it all.

Again that lion roared away out beyond the glowing fires of the watchful African police. Suddenly it was grey to the east. The grey became pink. I did not wait for the sunrise but went into the ward to take temperatures.

Witchdoctor first of all. It was down to 38°. I pressed the stethoscope against his chest. The turbulent sounds were gone. The antibiotic had beaten the infection.

I went quietly around the room, giving pills and water. A drum started to beat outside. It was the familiar rhythm of the early morning drum of the hospital calling people to spend the first of the day with God.

Simba and Mboga, who looked terribly tired, were outside the Chief's house. For a few more seconds Simba kept on beating the drum that he had hung on a post.

Mboga's fingers moved over his *ilimba* and he started on the old hymn, 'What a friend we have in Jesus, all our sins and griefs to bear. What a privilege to carry everything to God in prayer.'

The people sang heartily, then Simba's urgent voice rang out. 'The words of Jesus are these. "I am the road. I am the truth. I am the light. I am the resurrection and the life. I am the water of life. I am the bread of life." These are the words of the Son of God himself.'

Mboga had dropped his *ilimba*. His head was in his hands. Simba started to pray and I watched Mboga slide slowly off the stool and fall to the ground.

I went across as silently as possible. Simba finished his prayer. We lifted Mboga up. He looked at me with fever-ridden eyes. He held his ribs with his hand and muttered, 'I've got it, Bwana, the stabbing disease, pneumonia. This is how it always starts.'

Simba helped him across to the place where our microscope was. Suddenly he coughed. I clamped a handful of cotton wool over his mouth. When the spasm was over I examined what was on that cotton wool, stained it and looked at it under the microscope.

Daudi had joined us with Simba and Perisi.

'Do you see the germs of pneumonia, doctor?'

'No, but there are thousands of plague germs. Mboga has the same trouble as Pumba, but we've used up all the streptomycin.'

14

Plague Creeps Nearer

Mboga lay on a stretcher, a thermometer under his arm. Daudi counted his pulse, timing it with an alarm clock, the second hand of which was decidedly rickety.

He came across and whispered to me, 'Temperature 40°, doctor. Pulse 180.'

'Perisi, would you rig up another one of those beds with the special mosquito-net covering?'

She nodded and hurried across to begin her task.

Mboga looked up at me. 'Is it bad?'

'Yes, Mboga.'

'Bwana, is it not a good thing then that I swallowed those eight pills?'

'Truly wonderful. There was no accident about that. But here are another eight. Swallow them down.'

Mboga chewed them up and swallowed them. 'Bwana, will I recover?' he whispered.

'I hope so.'

'You're not sure?'

'No. I'm not sure. It is hard to know with this disease.'

He looked down for a minute. 'Would it be possible to send for my wife, Mzito? Behold, my heart calls for her.' He paused and coughed. 'But would it be safe for her to come? Might she not get this disease?'

'Yes, she might, but probably she would prefer to run the risk.'

I whispered to Simba. He went down the path that led to the police who surrounded the village. One of them would go and call her.

The witchdoctor was asleep, his breathing now at a reasonable speed. For him the danger was over. Relations of the sick people brought food and there was quite a bit of chattering.

I sat on a stool in a dark corner and started to pray. Tiredness seemed to press down on me. My mind switched across to a verse in the Bible, a verse that was a sort of cheque that could always be cashed. I prayed the words, 'They that wait upon the Lord shall renew their strength, they shall run and not be weary, they shall walk and not faint.'

'O Lord,' I whispered, 'this is an emergency, and if ever I needed strength and courage and encouragement, now is the time. Help me to run and not to be weary, and to walk and not be faint.'

On the windowsill were the four empty ampoules that had made the difference between life and death to the witchdoctor. If only I had some more of this drug! It could well be the only thing that would save Mboga's life – or my own, for that matter.

Perisi followed the direction of my eyes. She said, 'Bwana, if you do not sleep you will become sick. Examine the patients, leave instructions then rest.'

'*Yoh*, a bath is the thing I want.'

She laughed. 'Behold, Bwana, baths are hard to find in this place.'

We now had twenty-three patients, six of them seriously ill, the others, thank God, were improving. It took me almost two hours to examine them all and to arrange for their medicine.

I went outside. The Chief and Simba had the people hard at work. Bricks were being made to be dried in the sun for the building of new-type houses. As they worked they sang songs that had a built-in chorus.

I whispered to Simba, 'Would you bring a kerosene tin full of water? If there's one thing I long for, it's a bath. There is small work in putting up one of those canvas covers like a curtain under that umbrella tree and I'm going to have a shower bath by means of a jug and that tin full of water.'

Clean clothes hung on a limb above me. I took off my clothing after making sure that the canvas sheeting which hung from the limbs was secure. I stood on a flat stone and poured the water over my head, over my shoulders, over my body. The water was brackish and the soap wouldn't lather properly but it was a most satisfying bath. My relaxation, however, was somewhat spoilt when two small Africans suddenly lifted the sheet and peered at me, wide-eyed. As rapidly as they had appeared they disappeared and I heard one say to the other, 'There you are, I told you. They are white all over!'

I shouted with laughter. Simba arrived at the double. I told him what had happened. For the first time in days laughter rang through that village.

As I dried myself I was acutely aware of a soreness in my groin. The tell-tale lumps were there on the right. It is a routine medical thing to look for scratches, bumps, infections of toes, feet or shins.

There was an infected place above my ankle where a thornbush had torn the skin. Those glands could be quite ordinary or very deadly.

A strange flush came over me. If these swellings were caused by plague it could mean death.

I went to the microscope and followed the regular routine of germ hunting. It was decidedly uncomfortable to push needles into swollen glands, especially when they are your own. I was so engrossed in doing this task that I didn't notice the door move and a boy and a dog stop short. Carefully I withdrew the needles and swabbed the spot with antiseptic.

'Bwana,' Kisu's voice was husky, 'have you caught it too?'

In surprise I dropped the bottle.

'*Yoh*! Kisu, you startled me.'

'Bwana,' he repeated, 'have you caught this disease of deadliness?'

'Maybe. The swellings are there. I'm looking for *dudus* now.'

Stain was poured on the glass slide which would soon go under the microscope.

'Aren't you frightened, Bwana?'

'A little, Kisu.'

'*Hongo*, with me is terrible fear of dying, Bwana.'

'That doesn't worry me, Kisu, because there is nothing vague or terrifying about it. The thing that is called "the sting of death" is gone.'

'The sting of death, Bwana?'

'*Ngheeh*, the sting of death is sin.'

'Sin, Bwana?'

'Sin is a great wall built of the wrong things we've done. It stands between us and God. To die with that wall still there would be a horrible thought but… wait a minute while I put on the other stain.'

'Bwana,' his voice a whisper, 'don't talk. See if there are any germs of death in your body.'

'No use hurrying, Kisu. It takes time to stain. As I said, there's no fear when the wall's gone.'

Kisu swallowed. 'How did you break it down?'

'I didn't. He did.'

'He? Who is he?'

'Jesus, the Christ, the Son of God. He died to do this and now he lives so that whoever trusts him to take away their sins is able to face God without fear of his anger.'

'You trust him, like people trust you when you give them medicine?'

'Yes, it's very much like that.'

The small dog sat with his head on his forepaws and watched every movement as I dried the slide by waving it gently in the air.

'For years, Kisu, I turned my back on God. But one day words from God's book hit me like a knobbed stick. "How shall we escape if we neglect – turn our backs on – so great a salvation – cure?" Till then I had fear of dying, very real fear, but when I asked Jesus to forgive me, he did. Then everything changed, fear dissolved – disappeared.'

On the glass slide I placed a drop of cedar-wood oil, lowered the lens of the microscope and focused. For some minutes I looked carefully at the slide, moving it slowly and systematically up and down.

'Bwana, tell me, what do you find?'

'Nothing so far, Kisu. But suppose there is, see these pills in the big bottle?'

Kisu nodded and Chibwa wagged his tail.

'These are the answers to the trouble. Take them and you recover, leave them in the bottle and the disease goes on and on.'

I had looked at most of the slide and not a germ came into view.

'Nothing, Kisu.'

'Bwana, are you sure?'

'No, I'll do it again.'

The minutes crept by as I repeated the test. A second time I used the microscope with the utmost care. With deep relief I turned to the boy. 'Nothing, Kisu. It's only a scratch on my leg and is the work of ordinary germs, not the deadly ones.'

The dog looked at me with his head on one side and Kisu stood up. 'Bwana, I have prayed to God. This is the answer to one of the things I asked.'

'Thank you for speaking to God for me, Kisu! This is a thing of special importance. Tell me, did your prayer end there?'

'No, Bwana.' His voice was muffled. 'I made a large request for myself.'

'Which was?'

'You know, Bwana.'

'Tell me, for God's own words are, "If you tell with your own mouth that Jesus is Lord, and if you believe in your own heart that God raised him from the dead, you will be saved."'

'Bwana, I've asked him to forgive me and cure my soul. I believe in my very middle that he has.'

I put my hand onto his shoulder. 'That is the most important thing that can ever happen to you or to anybody.'

Fatigue suddenly seemed to descend on me.

'Kisu, there is much to be done. I must rest and gain strength for it.'

He nodded, and six feet moved quietly out of the room.

15
Bad to Worse

Ten minutes later I was asleep, quite unaware that midday had come and gone. Three o'clock in the afternoon likewise passed unnoticed.

At four Simba woke me. 'Bwana, you have slept deeply. Behold, here is food.'

'*Yoh*, thank you, but first tell me, how's Mboga?'

Simba shook his head. 'Bwana, his sickness is great.'

'He must have more pills.'

'He has had pills, Bwana.'

'We must also give pills to Pumba.'

'He has had them, Bwana. All your orders have been followed. Eat your food and relax.'

I did so. My groin glands were still swollen. I went through the examination again. To my intense relief no plague germs showed up and my temperature was normal. Then I hurried to the ward. Mboga's condition was grave. I looked up from examining his heart and lungs and saw at the door Mzito, his wife, a girl from whose shoulders we had removed a tumour as large as her head. Perisi was already fitting her out with the gown, mask and goggles that were so necessary to avoid contracting the complaint.

She went down on her knees beside Mboga's bed and took his hand in hers. He was unconscious.

'Bwana,' she whispered, 'will he live?'

'He is in the hands of God, Mzito. We know that the words of God are these, "Underneath are the everlasting arms." God is supporting him.'

'But will he live?'

'I cannot say.'

From the other side of the ward came the voice of Pumba, demanding food.

'*Koh*, am I to lie here without food? *Hongo*, it is a thing of wonder that the Bwana does not understand the ways of stomachs!'

Daudi's eyes gleamed for a moment but he quietly went outside and returned with a bowl of maize porridge.

'How am I know that it has no medicine in it,' sneered Pumba, 'medicine to take away my skill, to…?'

Simba stepped across to him and in a low voice that was hard as iron said, 'Silence, quieten the poison of your twisted tongue or I shall eat all your food, medicine and all, and the walls of your stomach will rub together without joy and your backbone will be seen through the skin beneath your ribs.'

Mzito hadn't heard the interruption.

'Bwana, why do these things happen?'

I shook my head. 'I have no idea. One thing I do know, God does all things well. He knows the end and the beginning. He can see the whole picture of our lives.'

She looked across the room at the four empty bottles which had contained the medicine that could well have saved her husband's life. Then she looked at Pumba, already petulant and demanding. In a choking voice she said, 'Why should he live, he who follows God not at all, he who lives with his back to God? And my Mboga…' Her voice caught. 'He travels the road of death.'

'I can't answer these problems, Mzito. They are beyond me. But I do know that God's book that cannot lead you astray says, "The steps of a good man are ordered by the Lord."'

I could not see her face because of the gauze mask that she wore and the dark glasses that covered her eyes, but moisture started seeping through the gauze on each side of her cheeks.

Quietly I spoke on. 'Do you ever think, Mzito, that if you and I had had the work of arranging Jesus' life for him we would not have agreed to wait until he was thirty before starting his work of teaching and healing and preaching? We would not have agreed that he should work for only three short years. How we would have opposed the thought that he should die a criminal's death when he was thirty-three, when he was still young, at the crest of all the possibilities of his life…so much not done, so many to be taught, so many to be cured. But God's way was that he should die.'

The girl held in her hand the *ilimba* which only the day before Mboga had used so effectively. She held it forlornly.

'Bwana, his fingers brought music from this and God's fingers brought music from him, but now it is all over.' She put the silent *ilimba* on the floor and tears ran down her face. 'If it is better for him to go and God wants him, what can I do but agree?'

'Do you remember, Mzito, when Jesus was in the Garden of Gethsemane, he knew that death was hovering over him. In agony he prayed that if by any means the cross could be avoided, that this might happen? Then he finished his prayer with the strong words, "Nevertheless, thy will be done."'

The African girl bent over her husband's hand. She looked at his normally cheery face which at the moment mirrored his dangerous illness. I heard her whispered words, 'O Almighty Father, I want him so much, so much, but if you want him more, your will be done.'

In delirium Mboga muttered, '*Ilimba*, *ilimba*, singing…'

'Who can play an *ilimba*, Daudi?'

'I don't know, doctor, but I will find out.'

He hurried outside and soon returned with Kisu, who took up the *ilimba* and thumbed it lovingly.

'Sit outside the door, Kisu, and play softly.' He nodded.

Suddenly Pumba sat up. 'Send that spirit-cursed child away. He plagues me with his noise.'

Chibwa's neck bristled and he bared his teeth, his muzzle wrinkling angrily. Kisu's eyes had a frightened look in them.

Simba stood beside him and whispered, 'Take no notice of the words of that one, nor let your small dog bite him lest his stomach be upset.'

Daudi caught my eye. I nodded.

He and Simba picked up Pumba's bed and carried it bodily outside and placed it under an umbrella tree.

'Lie there with your tongue at rest,' growled Simba. 'Later we will give you a new roof to sleep under.'

Kisu was playing on. Mboga was deeply unconscious.

Mzito sat with her head in her hands. The small dog moved over and put his head on her knee. She looked down at him and then across at Simba, Daudi, Kisu and myself standing quietly. Into her eyes came a look of deep thankfulness.

Kisu carefully put down the *ilimba* and, taking me by the arm, led me outside.

'Bwana, are the curses of the devil stronger than the powers of God?'

From far away came the howl of a hyaena to be followed in a few seconds by a roar of a lion.

'I'll answer that, Kisu, if you can answer me. Is the strength of the hyaena to be compared with that of the lion?'

Kisu smiled. 'It is an easy one. Surely lion is…' He checked himself and gripped my arm. 'Oh, I see!'

'We call him Almighty God because he is almighty.'

'Then why, Bwana, why doesn't he make Mboga better?'

'He can, Kisu, and we have asked him to, but is it for us to question his wisdom? Is it the Chief or the children who plan for the tribe?'

Kisu slowly nodded his head.

Three harrowing days passed.

Pumba was out of danger. He was able to sit on a stool in the sun.

'*Yoh*! he said harshly, 'the medicines of the Bwana did me no good. It was the special charm that I swallowed that saved me from this disease. The Bwana did me great wrong. Very many strong medicines were burned in my house. Much damage will come to him and his helpers because of this. It is for this reason that Mboga lies there dying and, truly, he will die.'

Four people had died, one of them a small girl.

Two nights before, I had sat beside Mboga's bed and heard Mzito talking to her. Mercifully, the little girl's mind was completely clear. In a way that no non-African tongue could do it, Mzito drew a word picture for the child of the coming of the Son of God into the world, of his mother and his miraculous birth, of his life and what he did for people. She told of miracles and parables, of how Jesus had taken the children and said, "Let the children come unto me. Do not forbid them for of such is the kingdom of heaven." She told how he had ridden into Jerusalem, the people shouting with joy. But three days later the same people had shouted at the top of their voices. 'Crucify him!' She spoke of his death, and I saw tears running down both their faces.

My own cheeks were moist.

She told how Mary had gone to the tomb in deep sorrow and, suddenly, in wonder too great for words, had seen the Saviour alive again. Mzito's calm voice went on, 'He, the living Son of God, who had conquered death, called her by her name.'

The African woman put her hand on the small hand in front of her. 'He calls you. He says, and these are his own words, "Come unto me and I will give you rest."'

'I'd love to come,' said the small voice, 'but I have nothing to offer him.'

'He is a Great One indeed, yet he asks no offering. He simply wants you, just as you are.'

The little girl looked up and said, 'Oh, and I do want to come.' Then she looked straight above her and said, 'Jesu Christo, O Son of God, I come.'

She settled down on her pillow and before long she slept.

When she awoke she was in the presence of the Son of God.

16
The Cure

In the late afternoon I sat in front of the Chief's house talking with Sumbili. He pointed with his chin towards new houses that were being built.

'A great thing has come to our village. New buildings, new ways of health. There is new hope.'

'Truly, Chief, new houses and new ideas are good, but what is necessary above all is new life.'

'You have brought it to us, Bwana.'

'*Eheh*, that may be so, but this is only life for your body.'

'Bwana, how can we have this new life for our souls?' Sumbili was on his feet pacing restlessly up and down.

'In our bodies you and I have the same trouble. We feel that tightness, as it were invisible bonds round our chests, when we get this disease, asthma. We both know the feeling. We both have no joy in it.'

Sumbili agreed.

'Right. You see that I have the disease, you know that you have the same trouble. You see I have a medicine for it. You see it undo the tightness in my chest and you want the same thing to happen to you. Then you come to me and ask for the medicine. See, in my hand I have it. It belongs to me.'

He nodded.

'I could give it to you or I could withhold it.'

He nodded again.

'I offer it to you. It is yours for the taking. There is no charge. There is no gift required. I put the medicine in your hand and in that second it becomes yours.'

'*Ngheeh*, Bwana, this is clear.'

'If the pills stayed in your hand they would have done your body no good.'

Sumbili smiled. '*Kumbe*, that is true. For them to work they need to be inside my skin and become part of me.'

'Words of truth, O Chief. Remember the first day we met? You didn't know how the medicine worked but you had seen it work in me. You asked, you received, you swallowed!

'For a while nothing happened. Your mind was full of doubt. Then suddenly you found freedom coming to your chest. Breathing became easier and *yoh*! You had joy.'

Sumbili's head nodded vigorously. '*Hongo*, this is truth.'

'One uncomfortable thing about this disease of our bodies is that it comes again and again. Both of us now have small bottles of these pills to swallow when we need them. This is a picture of the disease of our souls because sin truly binds us. You hobble cattle and tie up donkeys to keep them where you want them. Sheep and goats are put in pens for the same reason.

'Sin does this to people. It ties them down. It fences them in. See how this applies to you? You are alive but you are not properly free. You are 'sin-tied'. That's where the Son of God comes in. The words of the Bible are, "If the Son shall set you free you will be free indeed." Really free.'

I was remembering the time when I had heard Mzito explaining the way of life to the small dying girl. I told the Chief about it. 'There is the whole matter. He offers you this gift of life that goes on forever. You may do one of two things. You may refuse the gift, or you may take it as you took the pills from my hand and say "thank you". If you do this, realise that you have a new way to follow. You, a chief, have yourself a greater Chief, and his orders are to be obeyed.'

'*Yoh*,' said Sumbili, 'no more words, Bwana. I understand it. How may I take what he offers?'

'It is an easy thing to accept a gift.'

He nodded. 'What words should I use?'

'Everyday words,' I replied.

'Bwana, I will do it now.' He looked upwards and said, 'O Son of the Everlasting God, would you see fit to give your great gift to Sumbili, son of Nhonya, here in the village of Matama in the country called Tanzania?'

There was no voice in reply. There was no dramatic

happening. We sat in silence.

Then I said, 'Did he answer you?'

'Bwana, this is a thing of wonder. Nothing happened and yet, would God himself lie?'

'Indeed he would not. When I offered you a pill I didn't dangle it in front of you to taunt you.'

'*Yoh*,' said Sumbili, 'these are true words.'

We sat in silence for a long while, then Sumbili spoke again, 'Bwana, the reason that I wanted this thing was that I saw a difference not only in your life but in those of my tribe. The men and women who came with you, Bwana, they have this thing. It has made a great change in their living. Behold, Pumba has said hard words and received no hard reply. He has threatened vicious things and has received no anger, and I saw that you gave him the medicine that could have been saved for yourselves. Because of this, does not Mboga die?'

'And yet, Great One, when he became so very ill his wife was helping a small child who lay in the same ward, helping her to know the One whom you have asked to be your Chief.'

He nodded. 'Bwana, let me sit here and think of these great matters.'

Mboga lay under the protective net. Beside him sat Mzito in mask and goggles. Simba put on a mask and gown and stood beside me as I powdered up pills and prepared the small tube which had to be passed up Mboga's nose and into his stomach. He had been unconscious for two days and could not swallow. As I moistened the tube with glycerine and bent over him, his eyes opened and a slow smile came over his face as he saw the medicine glass with its white contents.

'*Yoh*,' he whispered, 'Bwana, have you nothing better than that for a hungry man?'

Mzito made a small, glad noise and stumbled forward, pulling the mask and goggles from her face.

'*Yoh!*' Mboga looked at her for a long minute with deep tenderness. He looked at us with the twinkle we knew so well. 'You understand, Mzito, even if the Bwana doesn't. *Hongo*, I have a famine in my inside!'

'*Koh*,' said Simba, chuckling. 'All is well now. He will recover.'

SAMPLE CHAPTER FROM:
JUNGLE DOCTOR
Spots a Leopard

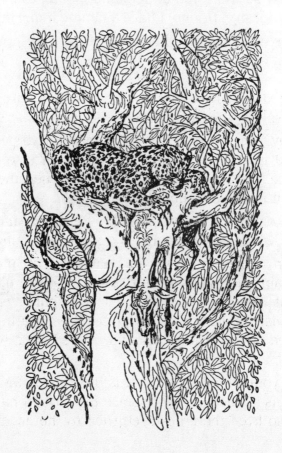

1

On The Spot

'Where did this leopard attack exactly?' asked the business-like voice of Yohah, the African Game Scout.

'Away over there.' The tall Tanzanian tribesman pointed with his chin and raised his voice to show distance. 'I, Yobwa, heard that it happened there to the south, near the village of Cibogolo.'

Now Cibogolo means 'witchdoctor's box' and was a place where violent things had been happening.

From a hair-pin bend on the road, cut into the mountainside, the two men stood looking out over the flat sweep of East Africa's savannah, with its thornbush jungle and baobab trees. In a clearing two hundred metres below was a flat-roofed, mud-walled house.

The young man spat. 'That is the house of M'sala. *Koh*! It is a place of death. Since the days of harvest, five who lived there have returned to the ancestors.

They…'

The Game Scout interrupted him. 'There have been words of trouble, of black magic?'

'*Kah*! Words?' Yobwa raised his eyebrows. 'Were there words? Great One, you know these affairs of witchcraft, when men of anger speak furtively behind their hands. And *hongo*! – then came this leopard.'

He shrugged.

'Have you actually seen it?'

'No, but one who saw it kill the new leader of this place said it had great spots like the bunched-up fingertips of a man's hand.' He dropped his voice. 'And the right forepaw is like this…,' he drew four dots in the shape of a square in the dust then rubbed them out hastily with his sandal, looking round as though he expected to be spied on. He moved closer to the Scout and muttered, 'The hand of Madole, chief of this village for twenty years, has but four fingers on it.'

'He no longer rules here?'

'Not even a little. In a night he found himself no longer chief, stripped of authority, and without power. *Hongo*! And did resentment and jealousy burn in his heart! It is said that he paid the price of many cows to witchdoctors, and a medicine of such strength was made to change himself into a leopard.'

The Game Scout spat. 'And who was given his place?'

Yobwa fingered the charms that were round his neck. 'The eldest son of M'sala. He had education and wisdom. *Koh*! But before a moon had passed, he was dead, terribly dead. It was the leopard with four toes that killed him – in the middle of the marketplace at high noon! This is not the way of most leopards. There are many who say that there is the cunning mind of a jealous man within that spotted creature's skin.'

The tall tribesman again looked furtively around. Yonah's face was mask-like. He ground out, 'Go on, – what happened?'

'Sickness came like a thunderstorm upon this house but death did not come fast enough to all of them. So again comes leopard.' He shrugged. 'It is a place of fear. All are dead there…'

As he spoke, out of the house below them staggered a boy. He stood for a moment peering up at them and then fell flat on his face.

The Game Scout jumped behind the wheel of his landrover. They skidded round the curves of the mountain pass, crashed through thornbush and bounced through huge elephant footprints in the black soil. Guinea fowl scuttled away screeching.

The landrover bumped over what had been a millet garden. There was room for only one wheel on the narrow path. Unexpectedly and forcibly the driver stamped on his brake. The man beside him shot forward, bumping his chin hard against the windscreen.

'*Yoh*!' he growled, 'Why did you do…?' his mouth flopped open. Across the path was a distinct line of white ashes. His voice was tense. 'Let us travel with care.' Both men jumped to the ground, and walked at right angles to the path, threading their way through the dead millet stalks. They peered at the ground most carefully before taking a forward step.

At last Yobwa spat in front of him. '*Koh*! The spell of death does not reach as far as this.'

Yonah grunted his assent and hurried across the clearing to where the boy lay.

Striding down the path towards them came a tall, cheerful man with a spear in his hand.

The Game Scout shouted, 'Stop! Look at the path in front of you! Stop!'

The new arrival paused, then deliberately scattered the ashes with his foot. He smiled, '*Habari* – what news?'

'*Njema*—good,' said the Game Scout automatically. Then he stretched out his hand. '*Kumbe*! It is Baruti!' They were both tall, solidly built men.

'*Eheh*, it is I, O Yonah Nhuti, and I have joy to greet you. Kah! But is there trouble here?'

'*Eheh*! Great trouble.'

Baruti bent and lifted the boy's head out of the dust. He was painfully thin, and his skin was burning hot.

'Is he dead?' Yobwa stepped back a pace.

'No, but he has much need of strong medicine.'

'Kah!' Yonah Nhuti scratched his head. 'I've been sent to deal with this man-killing leopard, and I find myself landed with a sick boy.'

'Let me put him in your machine and give him water to drink,' said Baruti, 'and perhaps we will find a way to help.'

Yonah grunted. He stepped confidently over the place where Baruti had trampled on the witchdoctor's medicine. He threw open the door of the landrover, and put a blanket under the boy's head as Baruti placed him down gently.

'You look after him,' he said gruffly. 'I will seek for the tracks of this great cat.'

Baruti saw that the boy was quite unconscious.

'*Yoh*! he cannot swallow,' he muttered, moistening the boy's feverish lips. 'Truly, he too is very near the ancestors.'

A shout came from the Game Scout, who was down on one knee in the dust near the house. 'Look at these tracks! A leopard has been here and walked right round the house, just as if it were a witchdoctor…and look!' He pointed to a group of paw marks.

'*Eheh*!' said Baruti, 'he lacks one finger in his right forepaw.'

Their eyes met. '*Hongo*!' said Baruti. 'You fear this creature?'

'*Koh*!' growled Yonah, 'any wise hunter fears any leopard.'

A cloud of dust was rising into the hot air two kilometres away across the plain. 'Let us drive to the road,' said Baruti. 'This is the bus to Dodoma and it will be the quickest way to carry the boy to the hospital. It will turn a safari of two days into one of two hours.'

At the hospital, we were having a special clinic to try and steal a march on tuberculosis. We had injected a drop of tuberculin into the skin of the forearms of a dozen people. I had just arranged with them when they were to come in again for me to see the result when Mboga, one of the hospital orderlies, came running round the corner.

'Bwana! Baruti, the hunter, has just arrived on the bus...'

'Has he, Mboga? Useful things, buses...'

'*Eheh*, Bwana. They take the weariness out of your feet, and shorten safaris truly...but Baruti has arrived, with a sick one. He says it is a matter of importance!'

Baruti stood in the shade of a baobab tree with his arm held firmly round a boy who coughed in a way that shook his thin body. The boy groaned and leaned back against Baruti.

'*Mbukwa*!' I greeted.

'*Mbukwa*.' The boy's voice was little more than a husky murmur.

'*Habari*?—what is the news?'

'*Njemi*—the news is good, but...,' he shook his head slowly. 'Are you the Great One here?'

'I am the doctor.'

'Have you medicines for the Great Cough?'

'Yes, we have many medicines.'

His eyes were bright with fever. He stood unsteadily to his feet. 'I have no gifts to bring for medicines.'

'Have you no relations?'

'In our house,' said the boy, 'were my father and my mother, my big brothers, and my small sister. But there was one who visited us, and he had the Great Cough, and *yoh*!...' He made a gesture with his hands and I realised that tuberculosis, like a bush fire, had swept through their home.

'Heeh,' he said, 'what can I do, Bwana? I have no-one. Evil has come upon our house.'

A bright yellow landrover came slowly along the road. Mboga, standing directly behind me, whispered softly, 'That is Juma bin Ali, Bwana. He is a new sort of medicine man and has been causing trouble with the ex-chief, Madole, who has only four fingers. It is said that he is trying to kill the old man with spells.'

Baruti gently sat the boy down with his back to the tree. He moved across to me.

'Bwana, he has small strength, truly. The only strong thing about him is his cough. You must help him.'

'We will, Baruti.'

The boy struggled to stand up, but his knees buckled under him. I picked him up and carried him the rest of the distance to the ward and put him into the hands of Mali, the trained nurse in charge of the men's ward.

'Put him to bed, and keep him quiet. I will come and examine him soon.'

'Yes, doctor.'

Baruti was squatting in the shade of the pepper trees.

'What is his story, O hunter?'

'His name is Tembo and, as he told you, death and trouble have come to his house. The Great Cough has struck again and again. Three days ago this boy, his elder brother and his father, all gripped by this sickness, sat in the sun as is the custom of the tribe. They live in a part of the country where there are many animals. Behold, through the thornbush stalked a leopard. He came straight at them. *Pow!* He hit the father and he died. He sprang at the larger boy, who rolled over and over, and this child fainted. When his

157

wisdom returned he was by himself. When I found him he had tasted neither food nor water for two whole days, and *hongo*! if there had been no bus, *kah*! he would have been dead by now.'

Baruti unslung his *ilimba*, sat down under the pepper trees, and started to play softly.

'*Kah*!' said Daudi as we walked toward the ward. 'He always plays that tune when he has sadness in his heart. And behold, today it seems to well up in him. Have you heard his story? He had four sons and all of them died from tuberculosis when they were young. There is great sadness in Baruti's heart. When he looks at Tembo he sees his own children all over again.'

'From the look of that boy, Daudi, I'd think that we're all facing tragedy. I wouldn't give young Tembo much chance of living even twenty-four hours.'

'Kah! Bwana, then he stands at the very gates of death?'

'He does. And our supply of drugs for this disease is desperately small. We need every pill and injection for other sick people. We have hardly any to spare.'

Daudi looked at me quickly. 'You're going to give him a chance?'

'We have to. There's more at stake than his body.'

This chapter is continued in Jungle Doctor Spots a Leopard.

THE JUNGLE DOCTOR SERIES

CHRISTIAN FOCUS PUBLICATIONS

Christian Focus | Christian Heritage | CF4K | Mentor

Christian Focus Publications publishes books for adults and children under its four main imprints: Christian Focus, CF4K, Mentor and Christian Heritage. Our books reflect that God's word is reliable and Jesus is the way to know him, and live for ever with him.

Our children's publication list includes a Sunday School curriculum that covers pre-school to early teens; puzzle and activity books. We also publish personal and family devotional titles, biographies and inspirational stories that children will love.

If you are looking for quality Bible teaching for children then we have an excellent range of Bible story and age specific theological books.

From pre-school to teenage fiction, we have it covered!

Find us at our web page:
www.christianfocus.com

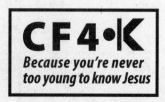

CF4•K
Because you're never too young to know Jesus